KIRSTY MURRAY was born in Melbourne and lives there still, though she has tried on many other cities and countries for size. She has been a middle child in a family of seven children, a mother to three and stepmother to three more, as well as godmother and friend to many amazing people. She has loved books, stories and people all her life, and is the author of eleven novels.

Other novels by Kirsty Murray

The Four Seasons of Lucy McKenzie
India Dark
Vulture's Gate
Zarconi's Magic Flying Fish
Market Blues
Walking Home with Marie-Claire

CHILDREN OF THE WIND
Bridie's Fire
Becoming Billy Dare
A Prayer for Blue Delaney
The Secret Life of Maeve Lee Kwong

THE YEAR IT ALL ENDED

KIRSTY MURRAY

ALLEN&UNWIN

SYDNEY · MELBOURNE · AUCKLAND · LONDON

Australian Government

This project has been assisted by the Australian Government
through the Australia Council, its arts funding and advisory body.

First published in 2014

Allen & Unwin
83 Alexander Street
Crows Nest NSW 2065
Australia
Phone: (61 2) 8425 0100
Email: info@allenandunwin.com
Web: www.allenandunwin.com

A Cataloguing-in-Publication entry is available from the
National Library of Australia
www.trove.nla.gov.au

ISBN 978 1743319413

Cover images: girl by Stevie McGlinchey, soldier by Ruth Grüner
Cover and text design by Ruth Grüner
Set in 11.3 pt Granjon by Ruth Grüner
Printed in Australia by McPherson's Printing Group.
www.mcphersonsprinting.com.au

1 3 5 7 9 10 8 6 4 2

To Julie Walker,

My Adelaide sister always

Contents

Tiney woke to the sound of voices drifting past her door. She slipped out of bed and tiptoed down the hall. Louis and Will stood by the woodstove in the kitchen, their faces lit by the flames that glowed in the open firebox. They were already dressed and Will had a bag slung across his shoulder. When they saw Tiney they grinned, their eyes shining in the gloom of the morning kitchen.

'Where are you going so early?' asked Tiney, rubbing sleep from her eyes.

'To Glenelg,' said Louis.

'For a swim,' said Will. 'Do you want…'

'…to come along?' asked Louis.

Tiney felt breathless in their company. For a moment she couldn't speak, glancing shyly from her big brother to her cousin. Louis and Will both had Wolfgang for their middle name, and ever since they were small everyone in their family had called the inseparable pair 'the Wolfs'. One of Tiney's very first memories was watching them wrestling on the back lawn, tumbling over each other like a pair of wolf cubs while she shrieked with excitement. In Tiney's imagination, Louis, with his thick dark hair, was the black wolf while blond Will was the golden wolf.

'How about it, little goose?' said Will, not unkindly.

Louis reached out and tickled her under the chin. 'She's my littlest swan maiden, not a goose, aren't you, Titch?'

Tiney slapped his hands away. 'I'm not a goose or a swan, and you know they don't let girls swim with boys at Glenelg Beach.'

'Don't worry, we'll be too early for the warden. Hurry and grab your togs. We don't want to miss a minute of sunshine.'

Tiney laughed and slipped quietly into her bedroom to dress, not wanting to wake her sisters.

The tram rattled down King William Street and on past Goodwood. Tiney sat between Louis and Will, dizzy with happiness to be allowed to be their mascot for the day. It was 1912. She was eleven years old.

The beach was dazzling; turquoise and blue water, white and gold sand with a few promenaders strolling along its length. The sea was calm and still, a mirror reflecting the morning sky. In the shadow of the long pier, Tiney changed into her woollen bathing costume and then skipped through the warm sand to where Louis and Will stood waiting for her, water lapping about their ankles. They wore identical black bathing suits though Will's skin had a honey-gold glow from working in the vine-yards while Louis was pale after a long winter of studying.

With Will on her left and Louis to her right, Tiney waded out into the cold waters of Holdfast Bay.

'Race you to the deep,' called Louis. He dove into the sea and Will plunged in beside him. A wave of icy water washed over Tiney.

'Freezing!' she shrieked.

Before she could let out another cry, the boys burst out of the sea and each grabbed one of Tiney's arms. They swung her into the air, over the clear ocean, up and up. Tiney would never forget the feel of Will and Louis' arms about her, the water rushing past her face, the sunlight cutting through the surface, the blue, blue sky above. She would hold the memory of the two young men, the air, the sky and the sea, like a perfect jewel of her childhood, for the rest of her life.

Tears of peace

On Tiney Flynn's seventeenth birthday, every church bell in Adelaide tolled, as if heralding a new year, a new era. Tiney stood in the garden of Larksrest, purple jacaranda petals fluttering down around her, and thrilled to the tumbling water-fall of sound. One by one, her sisters came outside to join her; first Nette, then Minna and lastly Thea.

All those bells tolling, the shouts and engine whistles, the beating of drums and saucepans on a warm spring evening could mean only one thing. Peace. Peace swelling up above the town and spreading across a deepening blue sky to reach the four Flynn sisters, as they stood beneath a jacaranda tree holding hands, willing the war to be over.

'Can it be true?' asked Tiney.

'The Kaiser's already abdicated – you saw the pictures in this morning's newspaper,' said Nette. 'It must be – peace at last.'

'They've been talking about the Kaiser's abdication for months,' said Minna.

'It could be a false alarm,' said Thea. 'We mustn't get our hopes up – let's not tell Mama, not yet.'

Nette laughed. 'As if she can't hear the bells! I'm going into town to find out everything. Right now. I won't sleep a wink unless I know for sure. Let's get our coats, Thea.'

'Someone should stay with Mama,' said Thea.

'We'll come!' said Tiney. She grabbed Minna's hand. 'Won't we, Min?'

'Papa will be home any moment,' said Nette. 'And he'll say you're both too young to be out gallivanting and then he won't let me out either. You all stay here, and I'll bring back the news.' She was already racing into the house to grab her hat and summer coat.

Tiney made to follow her. 'Let her go,' said Minna in a low voice. 'We'll take the bicycle. We'll be in town before she climbs off the tram and home again before Pa notices we're missing.'

The front door banged behind Nette as the others walked into the parlour. Minna bent down and kissed Mama on the cheek.

'Tiney and I are going too, Mama,' said Minna. 'You won't tell Papa, will you?'

Mama smiled and cupped her hands around Minna's face. She could never say no to Minna. Tiney sometimes thought Minna was Mama and Papa's favourite – for Mama, she was the daughter most like Papa, for Papa she was his wild Irish rose. Even when she was bad, even when they knew they should reprimand her, they couldn't resist her smile.

Tiney wheeled the bicycle down the side path but when they were through the gate, Minna took charge.

'Climb up behind me,' she said, as she steadied the bicycle.

'No! I want to sit on the handlebars so I can see everything. If you dink me on the back, I'll have to peer around you,' said Tiney.

'Can you keep your balance all the way into the city?'

'So long as you don't get too tired pedalling!'

Minna settled herself on the leather seat. 'Oh Tiney, you're such a scrap of a kid. I could pedal to Melbourne and back with you on board.'

'I might be small but I'm no baby,' said Tiney. 'Seventeen today!'

'You're still light as a feather. That's all I meant,' said Minna, pushing off from the kerb and sailing down the street.

As they turned the corner into Prospect Road, they dodged a brougham and two cars. The wind whipped Tiney's plaits out behind her as Minna pedalled like fury.

'Hold tight!' cried Minna.

They whizzed past tramstops thick with people, past slow, plodding horse-drawn carts and footpaths crowded with pedestrians. Thousands of Adelaideans were being drawn by invisible threads into the heart of town to hear the news they'd been waiting for these last four long years.

The bicycle hurtled across the bridge over the Torrens and along King William Road, and then Minna steered it into the park. They bumped down the grassy bank of the river and skidded to a stop beside a rotunda. Tiney's legs trembled as she jumped off the handlebars. Minna laughed and straightened Tiney's hat and collar for her.

'I probably look a sight myself, but you know, tonight I really don't care,' said Minna, smoothing out her skirts. Her cheeks were flushed, her hair windswept. She put a hand to her throat and laughed.

The two girls ran up to the road and locked arms as they made their way towards North Terrace, hurrying past the thick stream of people pouring into the city. Men and women shouted and yahooed all around them. Tiney and Minna were forced to stop as a procession passed by with three men on horseback and another young man carried high on the shoulders of merrymakers. Girls and young men marched along the street arm-in-arm, singing at the top of their voices while behind them a tin-can band made a racket and a woman stood on a corner weeping with joy.

'Now my Jim will come back again,' said a voice close behind Minna and Tiney. The sisters looked at each other at exactly the same moment. 'And Louis,' said Tiney. 'Louis will come back to us.'

Louis had signed up in August 1914, within days of the war beginning. Mama wept but Papa was proud, and his sisters thought Louis in uniform was the handsomest man they'd ever set eyes upon.

There'd been many times when the family thought he was lost, long months where they had waited for any word from him. Then Louis had written in late August to say he was coming home. His division was about to be rested and would set sail from England in October. Just the thought of Louis walking through the front door of Larksrest again made Tiney let out a spontaneous whoop of joy.

Not far from Minna and Tiney stood two diggers in uniform. The taller, handsomer soldier called out to them, 'It's a beautiful evening for an armistice!'

Tiney wanted to ask whether they had been in France, like Louis, and how long it had taken for them to be demobbed, but Minna spoke first. 'It's the most beautiful evening of my life,' she said.

The soldiers laughed. 'The peace isn't official yet.'

'I'm sure the Premier will be here any minute to tell us it's true,' said Minna. 'I feel so happy I could kiss someone!'

'Right-o,' said the soldier. And before Minna could object, he hooked his arm around her waist and drew her to him. Right there, while the crowds milled around them, Minna kissed him back. Tiney turned pink with embarrassment.

The second soldier looked at Tiney shyly. Tiney's heart began to hammer so loudly she wondered if he could hear it too.

'You're just a kid,' he said, as if to excuse himself from having to kiss her.

'I'm seventeen,' she said.

The soldier grinned. 'Well, if you're seventeen...' He stepped closer, sweeping Tiney into his arms. She lowered her head, bumping her nose against his bright buttons. They both laughed at their clumsiness.

As the crowds surged forward, Tiney wriggled free of her soldier's arms and grabbed Minna's hand to make sure they weren't separated as they wove their way onwards to the steps of Parliament.

It was 9.30 p.m. before the Premier arrived. Tiney stood on her tiptoes to see him but all he said was that there was no official news. If a statement from London arrived, it would be announced at noon on the morrow. The crowd let out a sigh of disappointment, but no one could shake the feeling that at any moment, peace would be upon them. Tiney and Minna wandered the streets, drinking in the waves of happiness that seemed to roll over the city. It was only when they heard the Town Hall clock strike 10.00 p.m. that they realised how late it had grown.

They pushed their way through the crowd and ran back to the river. As they stood on the bank of the Torrens, another roar went up from the crowds that thronged the city. Bugles sounded and songs of joy echoed along the river. Tiney and Minna hugged each other.

'This is the best birthday of my life,' said Tiney.

'Peace, kisses, what more could a girl ask for?' said Minna.

As Minna pushed the bike up the bank, Tiney asked, 'Was that your first kiss?'

Minna laughed. 'Ask me no secrets and I'll tell you no lies.'

'Minna!'

'Was it your first kiss, sweet seventeen?' asked Minna.

Tiney touched her face where the soldier's buttons and rough wool jacket had grazed her cheek. 'I didn't let him kiss me.'

Minna screwed up her nose. 'Aren't you proper? Well, don't you tell anyone about my kiss. Promise?'

'I may be proper but I'm not a snitch. Of course I won't tell.'

All the lights of Larksrest were aglow as Tiney flung open the front gate. For a moment, she stopped to admire her home; the golden sandstone cut square and smooth framed by neat red brickwork, with the four tall chimneys black against the night sky. The fanlight above the front door shone a welcome and the night air was full of the scent of spring. Tiney pulled down a branch of blossom and buried her face in the creamy petals.

'I don't think I've ever felt this happy,' she said.

As they stepped onto the tiled verandah, Papa threw open the front door. For a minute, the girls braced themselves for his anger at their going out without permission and returning at such a late hour. But Papa was grinning. He picked Tiney up off her feet and whirled her around. 'It's the best news in the world, isn't it, little one?' he said.

Nette was already back from town, setting the table for supper and smiling. Everyone was smiling. Even Mama was humming to herself. The mood was only broken when Tiney said, 'Do you think this means Will might come home too?'

No one spoke for a moment. Tiney winced, wishing she could swallow her words. Then Nette looked at Tiney sharply. 'Cousin Wilhelm is a traitor, Tiney. Of course he can't come home. He fought for the Germans. He might even have killed some of our boys.'

'But he was one of our boys, once,' said Tiney. 'It wasn't his fault that he was conscripted.'

'He could have said he was a conscientious objector.'

'In Germany? They would have shot him!' said Tiney.

'He's still a traitor,' said Nette, her cheeks reddening. 'He shouldn't have taken a German passport and Tante and Onkel should never have sent him to Heidelberg. There's nothing wrong with the University of Adelaide. It was good enough for Louis. Wilhelm should have stayed at home. But he chose Germany, and if he's dead it's because of his family's stupid ideas about *Deutschtum*.'

Mama put her hand over Nette's and took the soup spoons from her tight clasp.

'That's enough,' she said. 'I will not have you talk of your cousin and your uncle and aunt like that, Annette. Everyone, please sit.'

They were all seated before anyone realised Thea was missing.

'Where's our Dorothea?' asked Papa.

'She's in her cubby,' said Mama.

'It's not a cubby any more, Mama, it's a studio!' said Minna.

'I'll fetch her,' said Tiney, glad of an excuse to escape the dining table.

Through the paned window of the weatherboard shed at the

back of the garden, Tiney saw Thea sitting on a stool, surrounded by her art materials: tins crammed full of brushes, neatly lined-up tubes of paint, a white china palette, a small folding easel. It wasn't until she opened the door that she realised Thea was weeping.

'Thea, what's the matter? Are you feeling sad because you didn't come into town?'

'No, it's not that. I didn't want to go. I couldn't bear to see people celebrating when the world we used to know, the world we grew up in, is so lost to us.'

'But aren't you glad the war is over?'

'Of course I'm glad,' said Thea, turning her tear-stained face towards Tiney. 'I feel as if I've been holding my breath for four years, longing for it to end. But I can't stop thinking of all those boys we grew up with – dead or broken. All the ones that will never come home.'

Tiney put her hands on Thea's shoulders and turned her sister to face her.

'Stop it, Thea,' said Tiney. 'You mustn't talk like that. Louis is coming home, and Nette's Ray, and George and Frank McCaffrey and thousands of other boys.'

Even as the name slipped from her lips, she knew she shouldn't have mentioned the McCaffreys. Percy, the eldest of the three brothers, would never return. Thea looked at Tiney with her soft grey eyes and Tiney felt grief clutch at her heart, to think of smiling, laughing Percy dead and gone.

'Come inside and have supper with us,' she said, taking Thea's hand. 'We'll grieve the lost boys tomorrow and every day for the rest of our lives. But tonight, just tonight, we're going to be happy.'

2

White feathers

Tiney sat up in bed and looked out the window. Nette was gathering armfuls of blossom from the garden. Pink roses, sweet-scented and downy in the dawn light, were in bloom, and the first wisteria was budding on the side verandah. By the time Tiney joined Nette in the kitchen, every vase was full, every corner of the room bright with flowers. Tiney stood in her dressing gown and slippers and smiled.

'Wouldn't it be lovely if everything was in bloom when Louis came home? We could fill the whole house with flowers for him,' said Nette. 'We must start thinking of ways to make everything feel cheerful. I think we should paint the kitchen and put new curtains in his bedroom.'

'No!' said Tiney. 'We mustn't touch his bedroom.'

'Well, I was about to ask you to help, Martina, but if you're going to be cantankerous...'

'It's only that I don't want Louis to find anything changed.'

'But everything's changed, hasn't it?' said Minna, coming into the room behind her. 'Who knows what Louis will be like?'

'Louis will always be our Louis,' said Nette. 'I'm the closest to him in age. I should know.'

'You're not his favourite,' said Minna.

'I didn't say I was. He never played favourites.'

Minna rolled her eyes and looked at Tiney. 'I think Tiney was his favourite. She was always his darling. But he probably won't even recognise you now, Tiney.'

Tiney remembered when Louis used to measure her against the front fencepost and tease her about being like a fairy. He cut her name into the wood on her eighth birthday – Martina Agnes Flynn. Tiney felt her eyes swell with tears just thinking about it. She turned and walked away, down the hall to Louis' room.

As a little girl, Tiney used to hide in Louis' room whenever she was in trouble or unhappy. It was her safe haven. Standing in the middle of his room now, she could almost imagine he'd never been away. Everything was exactly as he had left it, though perhaps a little tidier. A square of morning light on the rug highlighted a faded corner of the blue wool. She thought of opening all the windows, but perhaps Mama would be upset. Mama loved to dust and air the room. Sometimes, in the evenings Tiney would see her, sitting in Louis' room in the dark, on the end of the bed, one hand stroking the pale blue bedcover, smoothing the fabric.

Tiney sat down on the patch of sunlight. It was cool in Louis' room through most of the day, so it was also her favourite place to escape the heat. She ran her finger along a line of books on the bookshelf. Tiney used to love *The Australian Boy's Book of Empire Stories*. When Louis had first gone away, she would lie on the blue rug in his room and thumb through those big, fat annuals, imagining she was going on adventures in India or Africa. Now she preferred the leather-bound volumes of poetry by German, English and Australian poets; Goethe, Schiller,

Hölderlin, Byron and Keats as well as Henry Lawson and Adam Lindsay Gordon. They sat alongside a collection of little books of quotes with silky-smooth covers and vellum pages that each of his sisters had given him. She took a volume of *Wilhelm Meisters Wanderjahre* by Goethe from the shelf and flipped it open to find Louis had pencilled a small star beside one line and translated it from German to English: *Das Leben gehört den Lebenden an, und wer lebt, muss auf Wechsel gefasst sein.* '*Life belongs to the living, and those who live must be prepared for change.*'

Tiney rubbed her eyes. She mustn't cry. Everything was about to change for the better.

There was a gentle tap and Thea put her head around the doorframe. 'Nette and Minna didn't mean to be scratchy. You'd better come out of there now and have breakfast. Nette says you both have to get down to the Cheer-Up Hut before your eight o'clock shift. She's got everyone's day completely mapped out.'

Tiney laughed.

The table was set for breakfast, with plates of steaming hot scrambled eggs and fried sheep's kidneys. Mama poured tea and handed around toast. Papa sat at the head of the table, reading the newspaper.

'Hurry up, Tiney,' said Nette, as she topped up the teapot. 'We have to get to the Cheer-Up Hut early if we're going to get away in time to hear the official announcements by the Premier. I'd hate to be serving lunch and miss it.'

'He's going to announce a whole week of celebrations,' said Minna. 'And I'm going to go to every single event.'

'Sadly, not everyone at the Cheer-Up Hut will be able to get away,' said Nette. 'Now that the war is over, we'll be busier than ever with all the men coming home. It's a shame more people in this family don't understand that and offer to pitch in.'

Minna didn't take the bait. She sipped her tea and then took her plate to the sink to begin washing up. 'What about your students, Minna?' asked Papa.

'No one's going to want to come to music lessons today!' said Minna. 'I can't imagine anyone will turn up for Latin or Greek either, Papa. We can all have a day off.'

Papa sighed. Tiney wished her parents would come into the city as well, but she knew Mama was shy of crowds and Papa would never leave her at home alone.

'Should we take flower petals to throw at the announcement?' asked Tiney.

'There's not much left in the garden since you stripped all the larkspur and the red and white roses last week,' said Mama.

'We had to!' said Nette. 'If only you'd seen, Mama! We stood on the balcony in Hindley Street and flung the petals into the air as General Pauc and the French Mission passed by. The soldiers loved it. There couldn't have been a rose bush or larkspur left in Adelaide with a single bloom. All that blue and red and white, just like the French flag.'

'Well, I don't think pink is quite the thing for victory, is it?' Mama said. 'So perhaps you can spare me my pink roses at least.'

Nette kissed Mama on the cheek while Tiney and Minna fastened on their hats. Even Thea decided to join the celebrations. The sisters walked together down the middle of Arthur Street in the bright morning sunshine. Nette with her pink cheeks and fierce dark blue eyes, her long golden hair wound into a bun, strode a little ahead. Unlike dark-haired Minna and Louis, Nette, Thea and Tiney took after Mama. Their skin was pale, their hair blond, their faces echoing the features of their Prussian ancestors. But since the war, Nette never let anyone say they looked like 'Rhine Maidens' – no one wanted to remember the fact that Mama's family was German.

When they reached the city, they disembarked from the tram together but Thea headed off along North Terrace to the Society of Arts. Minna was secretive and wouldn't say where she was going, except that she'd meet the others at the steps of Parliament House at midday, while Nette and Tiney headed to the Cheer-Up Hut.

Nette had been a Cheer-Up girl ever since Mrs Saeger had started the organisation to help comfort and support the troops back in 1915. Too young to sign on, Tiney had worked for all the Violet Day Appeals instead, selling buttons and badges on the streets of Adelaide and then waiting for Nette outside the old Hut behind the Adelaide Railway Station. By the time she was allowed to join, a new Hut had been built in Elder Park. She'd longed to wear the crisp white uniform and the wimple that would disguise her old-fashioned plaits. Mama insisted she wasn't allowed to put her hair up, not until Louis came home.

Tiney was faraway in her thoughts, imagining Louis standing on the balcony of the Hut when she heard Nette call out, 'Vera! Vera!'

Vera Destry was in her white Cheer-Up uniform too, hurrying across the dry grass away from the Hut. She must have been on the dawn shift. She looked at Nette oddly and kept walking. Tiney couldn't understand it. Only last week Vera and Nette had been best chums, resting their feet on a chair and sharing a cup of tea after a long lunchtime shift at the Hut.

'Vera!' called out Nette. 'Whatever is the matter?'

'I don't want to talk about it,' said Vera, thin-lipped. 'Not with you.'

'What's wrong?' asked Nette. 'There's no cause for anyone to be miserable! It's over, Vera. The boys will be flooding home! Buck up!'

'Nette,' said Vera, closing her eyes, 'I've just found out that I've lost my brother Tommy. He's been dead since September but the news only just reached us.'

'Oh, Vera,' said Nette, reaching out.

'Don't touch me!' said Vera, suddenly fierce. 'If it wasn't for you, girls like you, he would never have gone.'

Nette stepped back. 'What an extraordinary thing to say! He enlisted of his own free will. You showed me his photo. He was a strapping young man.'

'He wasn't a man. He lied about his age. He was only sixteen years old when he signed up and barely seventeen when he was slaughtered. I never wanted him to go. But after you gave him the white feather…'

'Me?'

'Yes, you. You told me yourself, last week, that you and that wretch Sylvie Pilkington would stand on the steps of the railway station handing white feathers out to every "strapping" young man you saw. Tommy was given three. Three feathers to a little boy of fifteen!'

'We wouldn't have known he wasn't of age,' said Nette, turning pale.

'I couldn't stop him,' said Vera, starting to sob. 'I told him he was too young. The first time he tried, they refused him, but then he ran away to Melbourne and signed up there. He would never have gone if he hadn't been made to feel ashamed.'

Tiney thought about Tommy Destry, a boy she might have passed on the street and looked at shyly, or sat beside in a school-room when she was small. A boy who would never be a man.

Vera's sobs convulsed her body. 'I raised him from when he was only eight years old. He was my little boy.'

'Vera, you must try to pull yourself together,' said Nette. 'You're not alone. Look at Mrs Saeger. She lost her son and she soldiers on. Don't let this spoil things.'

Vera looked at Nette with blazing eyes, her face suddenly contorted. 'Spoil things?' she said. 'Nette Flynn. Everyone knows you're half-Hun. You've spent the whole war trying to cover up your shame, trying to convince everyone of your patriotism. But you don't convince me.'

She shoved Nette in the chest and then turned and dashed through the park, tearing off her white wimple as she ran.

Nette put one hand to her cheek, as if she'd been slapped.

'She talks as if *I* killed Tommy! If I did give him a feather, it would have been because he looked like a great hulk of a man. How was I to know?'

Tiney slipped one arm around Nette's waist and gave her a quick hug. Secretly, she had never felt comfortable about Nette's white-feather campaign but she loved her sister too much to criticise her. 'Vera's upset,' she said. 'We can't imagine how awful it must be to lose a brother.'

Nette didn't reply. It was as if the day had grown overcast, though the sun still shone on the Torrens. They trudged towards the Cheer-Up Hut in silence.

The Cheer-Up Society

Inside the Cheer-Up Hut, hundreds of soldiers in the dining hall were joking and calling to each other along the length of the tables, but Nette kept her head down. Tiney felt a flicker of worry for her. It wasn't like brash, bright Nette to be so silent.

While Nette disappeared into the storerooms, Tiney donned rubber gloves, tied on a heavy apron and placed an upturned fruit box in front of one of the sinks as a makeshift step. Hundreds of plates, teacups and saucers from the breakfast service were piled high in crates. Tiney plunged her hands into the hot, soapy water and began to scrub. She only paused to look around when the back door was thrown open and a warm breath of spring air wafted into the steamy kitchen.

Ida Alston breezed in and flung her arms around Tiney as she stood at the sink. She kissed Tiney on the top of her head and laughed right into her ear, a bright metallic laugh that always made Tiney's head ring. Although Ida was Nette and Thea's best friend, Tiney always thought of her as the fifth Flynn sister. Tall, slim, long-limbed and impossibly glamorous, she was a regular guest at Larksrest.

'Oh, isn't it grand!' said Ida. 'I feel as if my whole world has turned on a sixpence.'

'It's wonderful, isn't it?'

'And what's more, Tiney darling, Mummy says we're going Home! We're going to England! And we'll go to France, too, to find our Charlie.'

Tiney knew how much it meant to Ida to see where her brother was buried. Charlie had fought with the 27TH Battalion and had died in the April Spring Offensive earlier in the year.

'Oh, and darling Martina! I didn't forget your birthday,' said Ida, reaching into her bag and pulling out a small parcel. 'Take off those ghastly gloves and open your present.'

Tiney stepped off the box, peeled off her gloves. With a flourish, Ida placed the gift in Tiney's hands.

'Hurry up! Open it! Open it!' said Ida, clapping her hands.

Tiney undid the silk bow and folded back green and gold wrapping paper. Inside was an extravagant black-and-green velvet scarf. Nestled amid the folds of the scarf was a framed picture.

'I drew it for you, specially. It's all my lovely Flynn sisters. I hope you don't think I'm silly but it's exactly how I envision your wonderful futures.'

Tiney studied the delicate pen-and-ink drawing, which was divided into four separate scenes. Ida put her arm around Tiney's shoulder and pointed to each of the scenes, naming the sisters. In the top left-hand corner was an image of Nette standing outside a grand house with a line of neatly dressed children. Beside her, dressed in a captain's uniform, was a tall, handsome soldier. In the opposite corner was Minna in a beautiful gown, whirling across a dance floor with a man in a tuxedo while a pretty little girl covered in ribbons and bows stood watching. Thea was shown sitting on a camp stool with an easel before her, painting a seascape; beside her, a man with a long, elegant face was also painting intently, and behind him was a large perambulator where, presumably, the artists' baby lay conveniently sleeping.

The fourth image was of an impossibly beautiful, gypsy-like character sitting at a small writing desk, her pen poised above a sheet of paper. A darkly handsome man in a beret lay stretched on a chaise longue nearby, reading a book to a small child nestled in his arms.

'That's you in your poetic future with your poetic-poet husband and exotic little baby. You're writing your magnum opus, of course.'

Tiney laughed. 'It's a lovely thought, Ida, and a beautiful present. I must show it to Nette. She'll be very flattered you think her Ray is so dashing, though he's not really a captain. She needs a bit of cheering-up.'

'How can anyone need cheering on a day like today!' said Ida.

A voice from the next servery called out, 'Ida, Mrs Wilson wants you to help with the flower arrangements.' Ida flew out through the swing door and Tiney plunged her hands back into the sink.

Trays of filthy plates mounted up beside the sink and when Tiney finished her allotted dishwashing, she hurried upstairs to help bring stores from the pantry for the soldiers' luncheon. The Hut was more crowded than Tiney had ever seen it. Only fifty soldiers slept in the hostel next door but hundreds of men had come from all over the city to discuss the armistice. Though it was still early in the day, the billiard room was crowded and the writing room was full of men talking and smoking. Outside on the balconies, soldiers sat in cane lounges, or stood in groups, taking up every inch of space. The scent of tobacco drifted into the gallery as Tiney loaded up a basket with stores from the pantry. She smiled at the thought of Louis standing beneath the jacaranda tree at Larksrest on a warm spring evening, the glow of his cigarette bright in the darkness. Soon, so soon, he'd be with them again.

A fresh batch of donated food had arrived from the country and Mrs Yemm was busy sorting what should be used immediately and what could be stored. Tiney and several other girls were sent down to the storeroom beneath the Hut, where dried fruit from Renmark, pickles, bottles of tomato sauce and tins of produce lined the shelves while dozens of legs of ham hung from twine looped across the ceiling. Tiney climbed a stepladder and cut down two hams to be served with lunch, lowering them carefully to the girl waiting below.

At 11.45 Tiney was given permission to join a group of Cheer-Ups who were heading to the steps of Parliament to see Governor Sir Henry Galway formally announce the peace. Nette wasn't in the group, but Tiney found Ida and they walked through the park, arms linked. Soldiers swarmed around them, hooting and calling out, jostling each other.

When they reached North Terrace, Ida took Tiney's hand and they broke away from the other girls, weaving their way through the crowd to find a place near where the speeches would be made. Beside a table positioned on the first marble landing on the steps outside Parliament stood the Governor, his wife, the Premier, the Mayor and members of the French Mission. It was hot and tightly packed near the steps and when a woman fainted from heat exhaustion the crush of people held her upright until she could be carried away.

Tiney wanted to cover her ears, the noise of bands, whistles, drums and shouts was so overwhelming. Very faintly, she could make out the sound of cannons firing in the distance, a signal that the announcements were about to begin.

The Governor began his speech and the crowd cheered at the end of nearly every statement. When he announced that at five o'clock the day before the Germans had signed the armistice, the shouts and cries were deafening.

Ida began to weep, her face in her hands. Tiney had never seen her cry, not even when Ida had told them of Charlie's death. Gently, she hooked her arm around Ida's waist and guided her away from the heat and noise.

As they wove through the crowd, Tiney heard snatches of conversation. The school examinations were cancelled. Twelve thousand school children were to march from Adelaide Oval to the City Baths. A young woman talked shrilly of the Victory Balls that would crowd the year's social calendar. For four years, most conversations in Tiney's home had revolved around the events of the past months. When they received news of Louis' movements, it was always months old. It was impossibly strange to think that every conversation from now on would be about the future.

By the time they returned to the Cheer-Up Hut, Ida had recovered. Another shift of workers was arriving and Ida chatted to them excitedly, as if she had been cheering rather than weeping a moment ago. Tiney went in search of Nette. She looked for her in the servery. She checked in the big kitchen where meat was being carved and in the small kitchen where women were peeling and cooking vegetables, but Nette was nowhere in sight. Finally, Tiney climbed down the stairs to the underground cellar.

It was cool and dark in the cellar. Huge cuts of meat hung from the rafters. Wire baskets full of smaller cuts and hundreds of sausages lined the shelves. Beside the marble bench on which slabs of butter rested, Nette stood hunched beside a crate of milk bottles.

'What are you doing down here?' asked Tiney. 'I've been searching for you everywhere.'

'I needed to be somewhere peaceful for a moment,' said Nette, straightening her wimple.

'What's wrong?'

Nette hesitated before she spoke. 'Do you think Vera will ever forgive me?' Her expression was more bewildered than questioning. There were two faint frown lines on her forehead.

Tiney took her sister's hand and squeezed it tightly. 'Of course she will,' said Tiney, though it almost felt like a lie. 'But I don't know if anyone is ever the same once they've lost someone they loved.'

'I've longed for peace as much as anyone,' said Nette, as if she were speaking to the air, rather than to Tiney. 'I should be allowed to be happy. We should all be happy now.'

Tiney felt a flicker of guilt. The Flynns were among the lucky ones. Louis was coming back to them.

Although their shift was nearly over, Nette and Tiney didn't go home. They shared a sandwich and then pitched in with the four o'clock shift to help decorate the hall for the evening's celebrations. Friends of the Cheer-Ups kept arriving with armfuls of flowers. Even Thea came by to help Ida and her team fold streamers and crepe paper to make bunting for the stage.

Lastly, Minna arrived amid a crowd of soldiers returning from the street celebrations and joined in making red, white and blue fans to trim the dais from which the patron of the Cheer-Ups, Colonel Price Weir, would make a speech. Tiney stood watching her sisters at work. *This is what peace will look like*, she thought, *everyone working together for a single purpose*.

That night, to hundreds of soldiers, volunteers, and their families, Colonel Price Weir made a toast, 'To the day after and to the boys still on the battlefields.'

The Flynn sisters raised their glasses high in the air. Every thought, every vision in Tiney's head was of Louis and of the day, so soon, when he would walk through the front door of Larksrest again.

News from the Front

Every window in Larksrest was thrown open to the December sunshine. Minna and Nette dragged all the rugs outside and beat the dust out of them. Floors were mopped and then waxed, furniture polished and skirting boards dusted and scrubbed until it was as if the house had shed an old skin. Mama rearranged every ornament in the sitting room and had one of Thea's paintings framed to hang in pride of place above the mantelpiece.

'It could be months before he's home,' said Papa, a little annoyed by the family frenzy of cleaning. 'He may have been demobilised but I don't believe he'd be in London yet. I've read there are boys in isolated trenches that don't even know the war is over, and German snipers still at work picking them off because they don't believe the peace is final. Louis may stay on to help. There's a lot of reconstruction to do out there and they may want his talents.'

It was three weeks since the war had ended, but they'd had no news of his movements. Papa pored over the papers every day, looking for information about Louis' battalion. Troopships carrying thousands of men were leaving Europe. The government had promised that the last Australian troops would sail from England by the end of July 1919. Some reports said the first to sign up would be the first to return, and Tiney's heart swelled with hope because Louis had been among the first to sign up back in August 1914.

Tiney couldn't bear the thought that they might have to wait until July for Louis. Every morning, first thing, she'd slip into his room and sit on his bed. Sometimes she would read a poem from one of his poetry books. Sometimes she took her photo of him, as if she could magically conjure him by sitting in his room and gazing at his image. And sometimes she spoke to the picture, telling him that she longed for his return, and that Christmas was only three weeks away so he simply had to be there to celebrate with his family, no matter how much he was needed in France.

Then, on a hot December morning, everything changed. Mama was coming in through the back door with a basket of shopping, eggs and plums piled high. The front door rang. It was Thea who answered it and called for Papa. Then Tiney heard Thea cry out and thought, *How strange her voice sounds. Not like Thea at all.* Papa folded his newspaper and disappeared down the hall. He came back a different person. Tiney barely recognised him as he stepped into the kitchen from the cool, dark hallway.

'Who was it?' asked Mama.

'It was Father Alison,' said Papa.

'But why didn't you ask him in?'

Papa didn't reply, nor Thea, who was standing behind him, staring at the kitchen linoleum. And then Tiney knew. She knew before Papa even spoke. And so did Mama. Because Father Alison had never come to call before. Because the Flynns were not members of his church, or of any church in Medindie. Because there was only one reason why Father Alison had come to their door. In Adelaide, it was always the local minister who was the bearer of bad tidings.

'Louis?' said Mama.

'We've lost him,' said Papa, his voice breaking as the words left his mouth.

For a split second after her father spoke, Tiney felt as though she was out of her body, above the room, watching the scene unfold. Mama crumpling, folding over and crying out. The basket falling from her hands, the eggs breaking as they hit the freshly waxed floor, the plums tumbling onto the linoleum, the blood-coloured juice staining the pale yellow squares, Mama on her knees calling out, *'Mein Sohn, mein einziger Sohn, mein Liebling, mein liebster Sohn ist verschwunden.'*

Nette coming through the back door, frowning with disapproval at their mother speaking German, not listening, not realising. Opening her mouth to admonish and then seeing Papa and Thea and Tiney, their faces frozen. Nette letting out a low groan and collapsing onto a chair, calling out, 'Louis, not Louis!' Minna following behind her and screaming, screaming as she stood in the doorway, then covering her mouth to stifle her screams before bursting into tears.

It was Tiney who moved first, who took Papa by his arm and led him to a chair, who knelt on the floor and put her arms around Mama and helped her gently to her feet. As if the spell was broken, Minna began gathering the bruised plums and putting them back in the basket, while Nette fetched a cloth and a pan to clean up the mess of broken eggs.

Then everyone was still, sitting around the old table, numb with shock. Papa's face was drawn, his mouth strangely loose, his head in his hands. Mama was trembling, ripples of agony shuddering through her.

Thea, ashen but calm, was the first to speak. She put her arms around their mother and held her firmly, as if to stop Mama from crumbling into small pieces. 'Father Alison gave Papa a telegram from the War Office. Louis died of wounds in a field hospital at the front in September.'

'He's been dead for *three months*?' said Nette.

Papa pulled a crumpled scrap of pink paper out of his pocket and laid it on the table. Nette seized it, smoothed out the paper and stared at it disbelievingly. 'Father Alison should have come in and comforted us,' she said, her voice small.

'What comfort can a stranger bring?' said Papa. 'I didn't want him in my house. There's nothing he could say that would comfort us.'

Tiney looked at her father. His blue eyes were glazed and his beard seemed more peppered with silver than she remembered. He looked like an old man, not her Papa, as if the words Father Alison had spoken on their doorstep had robbed Augustus Flynn not only of the dream of his son's return but future years of his life.

'*Ich will ins Bett gehen*,' said Mama.

'Don't, Mama. Speak English, please,' said Nette.

'What does it matter?' said Minna. Bitter, bitter was her tone, like sour limes. 'The war is over and even if it wasn't, there's no one to hear us. No one can shame Mama now. Not now we've lost Louis...'

Then the numbness descended again, like a shroud over the room. Thea helped Mama to her bed and Minna made a pot of strong tea, but when Tiney drank a cup it tasted salty, as if her tears and the tears of her sisters had tainted the brew.

Winged letters

Before he went away, Louis had carved a wooden wing and attached it to the letterbox. Every time even a card was delivered to Larkrest, the wing flew skywards. 'So you'll know that my letters are winging their way to you,' he'd said as he fixed it in place the day before he left Adelaide.

Before the news of Louis' death arrived, Tiney would sit at the window and stare at the letterbox for hours, even after the postman had been and gone, sailing straight past Larksrest on his bicycle. She liked imagining that a letter for the Flynns had been posted into someone else's letterbox by mistake and that any moment the postman would come cycling back, because there *had* to be a letter from Louis. And when the carved wing did fly skywards, Tiney would be down the path like a rabbit, the first to check the post. But since the news, no one watched the winged letterbox.

Back in 1914 and 1915, Louis' letters had arrived every few weeks. From on board the SS *Euripides*, from Egypt, the Dardanelles, England and later France. After he reached France, the stamp of the censor began to appear on the envelopes, and great sections of text were blacked out. As the war years dragged on, his letters grew shorter, his messages briefer. Sometimes there would only be a Field Service postcard. One year, 1916, they didn't hear from him for six awful months. Finally, Papa wrote to the Ministry of Defence, begging for information. When the letters began again, it was as if they were written by someone else, so removed were the stories he told. He didn't ask after anyone at home any more. It was as if he couldn't remember them, as if they had all become strangers to him. There was only the war. The war and the mud. The war and the men who fought it.

Every week during the war years, without fail, each of the Flynn sisters wrote to Louis. Then Pa would take all their letters and put them in a single envelope and send them off. They'd even sent one from all of them after Armistice Day. Tiney hated to think that Louis had never read those happy notes. She stopped watching for the postman. She couldn't open her letter-writing folder for weeks. The pale blue stationery was painful to look upon and, of course, since the news, the ritual of writing to Louis had died.

A week before Christmas, on a hot, airless afternoon, Tiney sat in the inglenook of the parlour window, trying to write a poem. She looked out and saw Louis' wing pointing skywards. Suddenly, grief pierced her heart so sharply she could hardly breathe. She got up and walked slowly to the hallstand and put on her gardening apron, as if she was pretending that it was the garden that called her and not the letterbox. She hadn't ventured to collect the mail since Father Alison's visit. Perhaps a deeper instinct called her. Because there *was* an envelope addressed to Tiney in the letterbox. A single letter postmarked from France. A letter in Louis' firm, copperplate handwriting.

It made Tiney's fingers burn to hold it. A fleeting hope that perhaps there had been a terrible mistake flared inside her. Perhaps Louis was alive. Perhaps he'd only been missing in action, not killed. Her first instinct was to race inside with the letter before she'd even torn the envelope, to wave it in front of her sisters, to spark some hope in them too. But her rational mind arrested her urge to share the letter. It would be cruel to ignite such an impossible hope and then extinguish it. Instead she sat on the front step of Larksrest, beneath the tiny portico verandah, feeling the coolness of the stone beneath her. She took her secateurs from the pocket of her apron and used the tip to slice the letter open.

Inside were four sheets of fine paper.

Dear Titch,

You've written me so many letters and I so few to you – it's time I set things straight. I'm wearing those socks you knitted. The green and blue ones, and thinking of you as I write.

This last twenty-four hours I've been at a post – a chateau very close behind the lines. There's a moat around the place and, despite the fact you can hear bombs falling all day, there's a swan on the moat. It's white and beautiful and it glides around the chateau as if nothing in the world is troubling it.

Last night I slept, or rather lay down, in the chateau wine cellar. At 2.00 a.m. we were warned of gas and had to put on our masks. When that was over there was Coup de Main and a tremendous noise; torpedoes and shells and glass falling from already broken windows as the chateau shook and rocked. But in the brief moments of silence I snatched a few minutes sleep and dreamt of you and Nette and Minna and Thea.

In my dream, you weren't girls but beautiful swans.

Did you know that when I was a boy, I used to think of my sisters as swan maidens? I was always afraid that one day someone would come and steal your feathery gowns and take you all away from Larksrest. You must be so grown-up now, little Titch. Do you still wear your hair long? You must never cut it. When I come home, I want to see those long blonde plaits flying as you pedal your bicycle through the park. Save me a little bit of the girl version of you. Don't grow up without me.

After the sleepless night in the wine cellar there is not much left of the ruined chateau – no doors or windows and not much roof. Rain is pouring in, half drowning the poor blokes on the first floor. Luckily, I am writing this in what must have been the chateau's library, a fancy room with the ceiling mostly complete, though bits of plaster are falling from above the long windows. It is sad to see these nice houses and grounds destroyed – presumably they were nice once. Now it's all desolation and ruin.

But you would love France, Tiney. Not this France – the one of mud and suffering – but the one that will grow green again once peace is made. One day we will come here together, you and I and all the family. When there are no more bombs we'll walk through green fields and picnic beneath a laurel tree. At least, that's what I imagine us doing, when I'm lying watching the rain drip through the broken ceiling.

I won't be here in the chateau much longer – perhaps until Monday. And then I'll be closer to the front again where there are no swans, nor even the ruins of buildings, but I will be thinking of you.

With love from your brother,

Louis

Tiney folded the letter carefully and laid it in her lap. She shut her eyes and pictured Louis sitting in the ruined chateau with the lonely swan, thinking of his sisters. The letter was dated two days before his death; it felt as if it had arrived from the other side, from a vale of shadows. She thought of Louis lying beneath the cold winter ground, on the other side of the Earth, far from everyone who loved him, and an instinct to find him, to find his grave, to be with him and see the place where he died swelled inside her so powerfully that she covered her mouth with her hands to stop a cry of longing escaping.

She looked up to see Nette walking through the front gate in her Cheer-Up uniform. A corner of her crumpled wimple poked out of her handbag like a broken bird's wing. Her face was so melancholy that Tiney couldn't bear to add to her unhappiness. She shoved the letter into the pocket of her gardening apron and jumped up to hug Nette.

Nette smiled and hugged her back.

'What was that for?' she asked.

'It was just for you,' said Tiney.

Tiney sat on the end of Nette's bed and watched her take off her uniform. She stripped down to her slip, her pale skin shiny with sweat.

'I wish I'd had a shift today,' said Tiney.

'No, you don't,' said Nette. 'It was unbearably hot in the kitchens. What did you do this afternoon?'

Tiney fingered the letter in her pocket. She wanted to share it, but she didn't want any of her sisters to be jealous that she should be the one to receive Louis' last letter. Some days, he was all they talked of, others they could hardly bear to speak his name.

'I wrote a very ordinary sonnet. I wish I could sell my poems.

I don't suppose writing poetry is a way to get rich. I wish I had a job and could earn some money.'

Nette turned to look at her and smiled. 'Why so restless?'

'Because,' said Tiney, only realising it as she said the words, 'I have a plan. A plan for all of us. I just need enough money to make it come true. I want us to go to France – the whole family. To see the things Louis saw, to stand together by his grave and say a prayer for him, to sit beneath a laurel tree and remember him. Oh Nette, wouldn't it be wonderful?'

Nette's eyes brimmed with tears. 'Tiney,' she said, 'What an impossible dream.'

'The Alstons are going.'

'The Alstons are rich. Join one of the Memorial Committees. That's all we can do.'

'It's not the same. Perhaps I could be a teacher? Then I'd save up, every penny I earn.'

'I thought you were going to be a penniless poet?'

'I could be a poet and a teacher as well.'

'First you'd have to sit the examinations for Teachers College. And even if you did get a job, you'd never be able to save enough for a single fare on a teacher's wage, let alone the fares for our whole family. Don't be ridiculous.'

Tiney caught her breath. Rage flared in her like a flame, but somehow she knew it wasn't anger but grief, that searing, burning pain that had tormented everyone at Larksrest since the news of losing Louis. She jumped down from the bed and ran from the room.

In the back garden, she scraped up a scattering of wilted jacaranda blooms and flung them into the parched flowerbeds. Even the roses looked bedraggled, their fallen petals rotting among the weeds. No one had touched the garden since the news.

Tiney knelt down beside a white rosebush and began pulling out dandelions. She worked alone, sweat dripping down her neck. Her hands grew raw but she tore at goose grass and clumps of oxalis until the sun moved low onto the horizon. All the while, her mind churned. No matter what it took, somehow, some way she was going to get her family to Louis' graveside.

Inheritance

On Christmas Eve, an uneasy silence settled on Larksrest. Papa and Mama had gone to the station to collect Cousin Paul, and Tiney wondered if it was because of Paul that no one spoke all afternoon. In 1914, Paul had been sent to Torrens Island, along with four hundred other German South Australians, and then to Holdsworthy in NSW where he and thousands of other detainees had spent the war years.

The quiet in the house made Tiney's ears ring. In other years, she'd stood with her sisters around the piano and sung Christmas carols. Minna would be at the keyboard, Nette singing loudest, Thea humming along and laughing at them. Then Nette would bring out a plate of fried sugar buns or gingerbread fresh-baked that afternoon, no matter how hot the day. There had been four Christmases celebrated in Larksrest without Louis, but Christmas 1918 would be the first without hope of him returning, and their cousin Paul was a poor replacement.

Tiney pulled open her bedside drawer and stared down at the present she'd bought for Louis in late November, before the news had arrived. She fingered the blue silk bow and thought of Louis lying lonely in his grave on the other side of the world with no memento from her, or from any of his sisters. A fat tear rolled down her cheek and landed on the red wrapping paper.

Minna and Nette lay stretched out on the cool linoleum floor in the side hallway, escaping the heat of the afternoon. Tiney sat down in the doorway of her bedroom, resting her chin on her knees, and said, 'I wish Paul would hurry up and get here.'

'I wish he wasn't coming at all,' said Nette. 'He should have been sent straight to Nuriootpa.'

'It's only for the afternoon,' said Minna, fanning her skirt to make a breeze.

'They shouldn't have let him out of the internment camp. Hardly anyone else has been released. It's an armistice, not a peace. They can't go letting them all out as if the war had never happened.'

'Nette, don't be awful. Paul is an Australian, not a German. And he's our cousin,' said Minna.

'He may have been born here, but Paul has always been a snob about *Kultur* and *Alldeutschtum*. You can see why they arrested him. He was so loud about it, so stupid to be trumpeting about German rights when there was a war on. Onkel Ludwig must have moved heaven and earth to get him released early.'

'They never should have locked him up in the first place,' said Minna. 'He was only seventeen. Like Tiney. He wasn't old enough to go to war. It would have been as bad as Tommy Destry signing up.'

Nette bit her lip and glowered at Minna.

'You used to like Paul,' said Tiney.

'I had to pretend to like him,' said Nette. 'But I always thought he was a hothead. What was he thinking, writing all those silly letters to the papers about British war crimes when the Germans had committed so many atrocities? No wonder they arrested him. Though I suppose it didn't help his case having a brother in the German army.'

Tiney felt as though the hall had suddenly grown too hot, the air stifling. She stood up, stepped over her sisters, and went in search of Thea.

She found her in the garden, painting in the shade of the jacaranda tree.

'It doesn't feel like Christmas at all,' said Tiney, frowning at the soft watercolour painting to which Thea was adding the final touches, as if studying it would hold back her grief. 'I can't believe there will ever be another Christmas again. Not a real one.'

Thea rinsed her sable brush and wiped the bristles clean on a painting rag. 'We mustn't give way to despair,' she said. 'We must hope that it will feel like Christmas. If we lose hope, then we have lost everything good, every last bit of Louis.'

Thea's face had grown paler and her cheekbones sharper. Blue smudges lay like shadows beneath her eyes and there was nothing bright or hopeful in her face, despite her words.

'Well, then,' said Tiney, 'I hope you'll win a prize with that painting. You should enter it in a competition. If I was the judge, I'd give it a medal. Are you going to hang it in the next exhibition at the Society of Artists? Someone is sure to buy it.'

'I'm only an associate member of the Society, Tiney. I can't tell them what to hang. I can only submit it.'

'If you sold it, we could put the money towards a fare to England. A second-class return fare is just over a hundred pounds. If we travelled third class, it would be even cheaper.'

'Oh, Tiney,' said Thea, almost scolding. 'You can't be serious.'

'But I am serious. You know I think we should all be saving up to go over.'

Thea was silent for a moment. Then she changed the topic. 'I thought I might give this one to Paul, as a Christmas present.'

Tiney sighed. 'Nette said we shouldn't bother with presents for Paul. She said he probably wouldn't have any for us.'

'One doesn't give presents simply to receive them,' said Thea.

'So you're pleased that Paul is coming?'

'I'm sure Tante Bea thought she was doing us a kindness and that we'd like to have a young man visit on Christmas Eve, especially this year.'

'He can't replace Louis,' said Tiney.

'No one can replace Louis,' said Thea. 'But Paul is our cousin and we should help him to fit in again. He's been locked away for four years. It won't be easy for him.'

'Nette says they shouldn't have let him out yet.'

'He was never a criminal,' said Thea. 'He was a prisoner of war. There is a difference.'

When Tiney opened the front door to her parents and cousin that evening, she was both surprised and disappointed. Paul seemed so much smaller than when she had last seen him in September 1914. His skin was bronzed and his light brown hair was streaked with blond, but there was something about him that was diminished, less imposing than she'd remembered. He sat on the edge of the sofa in the parlour and stared at his circle of girl cousins.

Nette shifted restlessly on her seat, as if ants were crawling up her stockings. Finally, she left the room to prepare tea and everyone let out a collective sigh of relief that there hadn't been a fiery argument. But when she came back with a tray of buns, she lit the fuse.

'Would you like a Kitchener bun?' asked Nette, offering Paul a plate stacked with sugar-coated buns oozing jam and cream.

'*Berliner,*' said Paul, taking one from the platter and setting it on a smaller plate.

'We call them Kitchener buns now, and so should you.'

'Why would you want to name anything this delicious after the man who invented the concentration camp? The man who was responsible for all those deaths at Gallipoli?'

'He was a war hero,' said Nette, slamming the plate of buns down on the table.

'He was a British warmongering imperialist,' said Paul.

'You're a fine one to criticise imperialism after all that waffle you wrote about the Kaiser.'

Paul snorted. 'I was a boy when I wrote that. I'm a socialist now. Capitalist imperialism pits the workers of one country against another and profits on war. The only way to end war is to embrace socialism.'

Paul shifted to the edge of his seat and glared up at Nette as she stood over him, hands on her hips.

'Did you learn all that on your holiday in the internment camp?' snapped Nette. 'While our boys were dying at the hands of the Germans?'

'Children, please!' said Mama, raising her hands in alarm. 'We must have no more talk of war or politics. We are family, it is Christmas. *Bitte!*'

Nette was so startled at Mama's outburst she forgot to scold her for speaking German. Silence hung in the air like a cloud of sour smoke. Nette sat down, her arms folded across her chest.

Paul's gaze skittered across the faces of his cousins and then he sighed and stared at the ceiling. Tiney stood up and excused herself from the room. She returned with the book of poetry she had bought for Louis. She smoothed the silk ribbon and handed the gift to Paul.

'Merry Christmas, Paul,' she said.

Paul looked at her quizzically. 'Thank you, little cousin.'

He untied the blue ribbon and folded back the wrapping paper, then smiled as he read the title of the book printed in soft brown against a pale green cloth cover, *The Passionate Heart*.

'It's a book of poetry, by Mary Gilmore. I hope you like it. She's very fierce and I think she's a socialist too, just like you.' Tiney was suddenly conscious of how many poems in the book were about the war. 'One of my favourite reads, "*The fruit is never the tree, The singer is never the song.*" It's called "Inheritance".'

Paul looked at Tiney as if he'd just seen something in her that he'd never noticed before. '*Danke*,' he said. '*Wir dürfen nie unser gemeinsames Erbe vergessen.*'

Nette pursed her lips. 'Cousin, we are Australians and we do not speak German at home.'

Paul laughed bitterly. 'Don't worry. It's only illegal in public places.'

'Let's not start again,' said Nette. 'Can't you put the past behind you?'

'Annette, do you know how many homes of innocent German-Australians were set alight and businesses looted because of their "past" – their German ancestry? What about the thugs who burnt down the Lutheran churches at Edithburg and Netherby? Did you know Dieter Gebel enlisted to stop his mother and father being persecuted? The authorities took him but they still tormented his parents. Dieter's dead now. The warmongers wanted all our young farmers.'

'But *you* didn't have to face the trenches, did you, Paul? You spent the war in comfort.'

'Comfort? Have you already forgotten what happened on Torrens Island?'

Paul rolled up his right trouser leg. The older girls turned away, averting their gaze, but Tiney stared hard. Purple scars covered the back of Paul's calves, like strange, dried sea slugs, dark against his white flesh.

'Look at it,' he said. 'That's the sort of comfort they showed us with their bayonets.'

'Please,' said Mama. 'Cover it up, Paul.'

It felt like the longest afternoon of Tiney's life. Everyone was relieved when the doorbell rang and Papa opened the door to Onkel Ludwig, who had driven down from the Barossa to collect his son. Tiney heard their deep voices murmuring from underneath the portico and then Papa let out a low moan. Tiney ran to the door. Onkel Ludwig and Papa were embracing, as if they were holding each other up.

'Papa, Onkel,' said Tiney, afraid.

Papa kept one arm around Onkel Ludwig, supporting him. As he turned to Tiney, she saw his face was streaked with tears.

'Your uncle has just had news from the Red Cross,' said Papa. 'Your cousin Will died at Ypres in April. Both our wolf cubs are lost to us.'

The McCaffreys return

The floorboards in the front hallway of Larksrest had a hard, glossy black finish. When no one was around to see her, Tiney still liked to make a running leap in her stockinged feet and glide along the slippery boards. When the doorbell rang on a January afternoon, she slid down the last few metres of hall and opened the door to the youngest McCaffrey brother. It was three years since she'd seen Frank and it took a moment for her to recognise him. He was dressed in civvies: a clean-cut, pin-striped suit, a grey fedora hat and shiny black shoes.

He took off his hat and made a little bow. 'Hello, Tiney Flynn,' he said. He glanced down at her stockinged feet. 'I hope you and your sisters are at home to visitors?'

Tiney remembered Minna once saying, 'No girl could say no to a McCaffrey,' and she smiled shyly.

Before the war there had been a McCaffrey brother for three of the Flynn sisters. Tiney used to count them off on her fingers. Percy for Nette, George for Minna, and Frank for Thea. Mrs McCaffrey had fretted that the Flynn girls would steal all her sons. In the end, it wasn't the Flynn girls who stole her boys away from her but the war.

'When did you get home?' asked Tiney. 'Me and Nette, we've been watching out for you and George at the Cheer-Up Hut.'

'We're here for you to cheer us up right now,' said Frank. 'Got home three days ago. Me and George both.'

That's when Tiney realised Frank wasn't alone. Standing at the bottom of the front steps was Frank's older brother, George. How had she not noticed him? He was still in uniform, as if he had come straight from the barracks, as if he would always be a soldier.

'Hello there, Bubs,' he said, climbing the steps. 'I'd like to say you've grown since I saw you last but you're still a little squirt, aren't you?'

'Actually, I'm seventeen,' she said.

George simply stared at her. Tiney wished she'd kept her shoes on. She felt twelve years old again, looking up into George McCaffrey's blue, blue eyes. They seemed bigger and glassier than she remembered. There was something hypnotic about George.

'Any of your sisters at home?' he asked, at last.

'A couple,' she said, unable to look away from George's face. 'Minna! Thea! Guess who's here?'

Minna came up behind her, shielding her eyes against the light.

'George and Frank,' said Minna, almost as though she were disappointed.

'Don't leave our guests standing on the doorstep like a pair of travelling salesmen,' said Thea, hurrying up the hallway. 'It's good to see you home.'

They led the McCaffreys into the parlour where Mama was sitting on the sofa. She laid her embroidery hoop to one side and stood to greet the boys.

'Welcome, Francis and George,' she said stiffly. 'Your mother must be so happy to have you home.' There was something brittle, too composed, about Mama's politeness, as if the presence of young men in the parlour made Louis' absence more painful than ever.

Thea brought tea and slices of seed cake and set the tray on the sideboard, and Tiney helped serve the guests.

George kept fiddling with his cup, lifting it up, putting it back on the saucer, switching hands, as if he couldn't decide how best to hold it. When he wasn't fiddling, just holding the cup, it rattled slightly. Tiney couldn't understand why his hands were trembling. How could George, smooth, handsome George, possibly be nervous?

Before the McCaffrey boys went away, George had been the one that everyone secretly loved. Poor, dead Percy had been tall and kind but George had been dashing, while Frank was forever in his older brothers' shadows, waiting to be noticed. Tiney liked him for that, the way he was always good-humoured though he was often overlooked.

'And now that you're home, what are your plans?' asked Mama politely.

'Oh Ma, they're only just off the boat,' said Minna. 'They shouldn't have to know the answer to that question.'

George shrugged. 'I'll take whatever I'm offered. If anyone will have me.'

'Of course everyone will have you,' said Mama. 'Everyone wants our boys to get straight back to work, in good jobs.'

'I'm going to try for the civil service,' said Frank, running his fingers around his hat.

Tiney felt confused, as if they had all walked through a

mirror where everything was backwards. Frank seemed so much more at ease than before, while George's gaze flicked back and forth across the room from Minna to Thea to Tiney, as if he were trying to remember who they were exactly. Then he turned his focus on Minna.

'Oi there, Minna, you fancy coming to the pictures with me?' he asked, as if they were alone in the room.

Minna smiled, a tiny curve of her lips, but she looked to Thea, not George. 'Frank should come along too. And Thea,' she said. 'We could make it doubles.'

Thea raised her eyebrows. 'We should take Tiney as well.'

'Righto,' said Minna. 'That would be fun, wouldn't it? Your very own gang of Cheer-Up girls.'

George blinked, visibly annoyed. He slapped his hand against his knee and looked at the floor. 'If you must, bring the whole damn family. Whole bloody lot of you.'

'George,' said Frank, putting his hand on his brother's shoulder and glancing at Mama apologetically.

'Nette could join you as a chaperone,' said Mama, as if she hadn't noticed George's rudeness. 'Her fiancé, Ray Staunton, is due home any day now.'

'Nette's getting hitched?' said George. 'Got over Percy pretty quickly, didn't she?'

There was another awkward silence.

'We were sorry to hear about Louis,' said Frank. 'He was a great bloke.'

Mama nodded, as if she could not speak another word. But Minna turned and gazed at Frank with gratitude. 'Thank you, Frank. We miss Percy too.'

On the evening of their trip to the picture show, Tiney stood in the bedroom buttoning her summer coat. It was really too warm to wear it but she didn't want Frank to think she was under-dressed in her simple black cotton dress. She scowled at her reflection as she stood beside Minna in front of the mirror. Minna looked stunning in a very simple smoke-grey dress with a white collar. Tiney noticed its hem fell only just below her knees, revealing Minna's beautifully turned ankles.

'Aren't you going to wear a coat?' asked Tiney.

'I've a shawl,' said Minna. 'Let's not fuss. It's only the pictures. No one can see us in the dark anyway.'

'Papa says we shouldn't be going at all. He's worried we'll catch the Spanish Influenza.'

'Papa loves to worry. There are no cases in Adelaide yet and the Health Department says they won't close the picture palaces as long as they're disinfected every morning, so it must be safe. I think Papa's more worried about the McCaffrey brothers than the flu epidemic. He'd refuse permission if it weren't for the fact they've just come back from the war. You have to admit, George is a little frightening.'

'The epidemic frightens me a lot more than George McCaffrey. This morning's paper says millions of people are dying from it all around the world.'

'Stop it, Tiney!' said Minna. 'After all these years of worrying about the war do we have to talk about more death and destruction?'

At that moment, Nette and Ida burst into the room and flung themselves on the bed, laughing.

'Are you chaperoning us too?' asked Tiney.

'Absolutely,' said Ida. 'Keeping an eye on you lot is too much responsibility for poor little Nette.'

'I can't imagine George will like us so thoroughly out-numbering him,' said Minna.

'He should be grateful to have five gorgeous women in his company,' said Ida. 'And doesn't Minna look exquisite! I'm so glad to see you've given up on black. The prices being charged for it are ridiculous and besides, Adelaide has been awash with women in mourning for far too long.'

Then Ida caught Tiney's look of disappointment, as she pulled the collar of her coat higher to disguise her black dress. 'I didn't mean you, Tiney. You look like a lovely French schoolgirl, not a drab widow.'

When the doorbell rang, the girls hurried into the hall. It felt odd outnumbering the boys. But then that was how it was going to be from now on, thought Tiney, two girls for every boy. Nette and Ida each held Tiney's hands and hung back so that George offered his arm to Minna while Frank escorted Thea.

'Why are we bringing up the rear?' asked Tiney, wishing the men could have a girl on each arm.

'Because it's the right thing to do,' said Nette. 'Ray will be home soon. I don't need to be on any boy's arm. And you're still too young to even be thinking about having a beau.'

Tiney thought briefly of the soldier on Armistice Day who had tried to kiss her, and smiled to herself. Then a terrible thought gripped her. What if that was as close to a kiss as she'd ever get? What if the man who was destined to love her was lying dead beneath the cold mud of France or Belgium or beneath the cliffs at Gallipoli?

'As for me,' said Ida, interrupting Tiney's thoughts, 'I'm holding out for a dashing European or a charming member of the English gentry.'

'When are you going over to France?' asked Tiney.

'We've had to put our plans on hold until the flu epidemic eases,' said Ida. 'People are dying like flies in England and there are so many ships in quarantine that we can't leave. It seems we'll be waiting forever.'

'Not forever,' said Tiney. 'Who knows? Maybe by the time the flu epidemic has passed, we'll be going too.'

Ida glanced at her, bemused, and Tiney realised Nette must have told her of Tiney's impossible dream.

They climbed off the tram at the corner of North Terrace and then sauntered along Peel Street and into Hindley Street. The Wondergraph was lit up with a thousand electric lights. Frank said it was the most opulent picture palace in the whole country, and Tiney could believe it. George and Frank bought tickets while the girls stood together in the bright foyer.

It was strangely empty inside the theatre. It smelt so strongly of disinfectant that Tiney's eyes stung. Hundreds of seats were vacant. Some people were wearing cloth masks over their mouths and when a man sitting in the front row coughed into his hand-kerchief, the people next to him stood up and changed seats. Then the orchestra struck up the overture and the lights dimmed.

There were two short films before the opening credits of the main feature. A line of beautiful young women danced across the screen and then threw off their gowns to reveal close-fitting bathing suits and bare arms and legs.

Tiney leaned over and whispered into Nette's ear. 'I thought we were going to see Charlie Chaplin!'

'That's showing at the Pavilion,' said Nette. 'George insisted we see this instead. He's mad about Mack Sennet's movies.'

Tiney knew Papa wouldn't be happy about George's choice. The movie was called *Ladies First* but there was nothing polite about the way the actors behaved. Bathing beauties danced on beaches, handsome men in tailored suits lounged in bars admiring bare-shouldered women in satin gowns in a world far removed from the quiet of Larksrest.

Suddenly, Minna laughed aloud and Tiney saw her lean forward in her seat. A curl of hair lay dark against her white neck and her face looked so beautiful in profile, so much lovelier than any of the women on the silver screen, that Tiney smiled. In the same instant, she felt a flicker of unease. She wasn't the only one admiring Minna in the half-light. George was gazing at her too, his pale eyes strangely empty in the flickering light from the screen. He slipped one arm around the back of Minna's seat but then caught sight of Tiney watching him, scowled and withdrew it.

Tiney was glad when the film was over and they could escape the theatre and breathe the warm evening air outside. Soldiers wandered the city streets, some with laughing women on their arms, some alone. One stood on the corner of Rundle and King William Street, singing 'On the Road to Gundagai' with his slouch hat held out in front of him. Tiney felt embarrassed when she realised he was supporting himself with a crutch. It was less than three months since the war had ended. How could a war hero have to sing for his supper? Frank stopped and took a shilling out of his pocket and put it in the busker's hat. Then he took his hat off, as if in solidarity.

'Thanks, cobber,' said the soldier.

The five girls walked slowly to the tramstop while George

strode ahead. Tiney glanced back. Frank and the singing soldier had their heads inclined towards each other, their faces sombre. In the gold and orange glow of the streetlight Frank's hair shone like copper. Tiney had never noticed how handsome he was before.

When Frank caught up with them he began to apologise.

'There's nothing to apologise for,' said Minna, resting her hand lightly on his arm.

'He was a good bloke, that soldier. He fought at Bullecourt but spent the last year in Blighty, in an English hospital. Poor fellow lost his leg but now he's having trouble getting a pension. They reckon he's able-bodied and should be working.'

George laughed, that dry, angry bark that Tiney had noticed when he'd come to visit them at Larkspur. 'There are plenty of stronger men who can't find employment. He's better off on the street.'

'George,' said Nette, 'my Ray has taken up land at Cobdolga with the soldier settlement scheme. You should look into it.'

George looked at Nette darkly. 'Your Ray is a mug. Percy would never have signed up for that rort.'

Nette blanched. She had wept every night for months after Percy died at Gallipoli, and no one spoke his name in front of her any more. Frank stepped between his brother and Nette, and Tiney looked for the lights of the tram, as if for a ray of hope in the darkness.

Keeping promises

Mama was on the telephone, chatting in German to Tante Bea, when Nette and Tiney came into the hall to hang their coats and hats after a morning shift at the Cheer-Up Hut. Tiney was pleased. It had taken their mother a very long time to become accustomed to using the daunting black box. But Nette was furious.

'Ma! Don't you read the papers!'

Mama stopped speaking mid-sentence and looked up in surprise. Nette took the receiver from her mother and spoke directly into the phone. 'Auntie Bea – you can't speak German on the telephone to Ma. And she can't speak it to you. They've banned it. War precautions – it was in the paper last month. No one is to speak German on the phone. The operators at the exchange will report you!' Then Nette hung up.

Ma sighed. 'But the war is over.'

'Not until the Germans sign a treaty. It's only an armistice until then.'

Mama gave Nette one of her faraway looks, an expression that they saw all too often now.

'Why don't you come out with us to the station to meet the train this afternoon?' asked Tiney, gently.

Mama shook her head. 'I have to finish my embroidery,' she said. She gathered up her sewing basket and went to sit in the parlour. More and more of Mama's days were consumed with embroidering small sayings onto offcuts of black cloth left over after Minna had made everyone's mourning dresses. Since the news, Mama had changed. New lines had appeared around her mouth and eyes, like hairline fractures. It was as if, on that day when she fell to the kitchen floor, something deep inside her had torn apart and no matter how many embroidery samplers she made, nothing could stitch shut the wounds.

Tiney leaned over her shoulder and read the newest quote. *'In the far graves the voices break: He is asleep; he will not wake.'*

'Oh, that's from Mary Gilmore's poem, isn't it?'

Mama nodded and handed a copy of the poem to Tiney. It had been carefully cut from a newspaper.

'This was is in the book of poetry that I gave to Paul,' said Tiney, scanning the lines of 'These Fellowing Men', a poem about young soldiers buried in European graves. Emboldened, she knelt down beside her mother. 'Mama, I have an idea. It's something for Louis. I've been thinking and thinking about it. We should all go to France together, to find his grave.'

Unexpectedly, Mama laughed. She put one hand on Tiney's head and stroked her fair hair. *'Liebchen*, this is an impossible dream.'

'It doesn't have to be impossible. The Alstons are going. We could go too!'

Mama frowned and picked up her embroidery. 'No, Martina. We must hope they send him home to us.'

'But they won't send him home! *That's* impossible. Tens of thousands of men died, Mama. They won't send any of them home. Please, Mama. We could draw on your trust fund. We could all go before Nette gets married.'

'Martina! *Das reicht jetzt!*'

Mama only called Tiney by her full name when she was angry, and only spoke to her daughters in German when she was distressed. Tiney had never heard her speak with such rage to anyone.

Tiney ran to her room and flung herself onto her bed, sobbing. Minna came into the room and sat on the edge of the bed and stroked her back.

'What's the matter, Tiney? What's happened?'

Tiney sat up and rubbed her tear-stained face. 'Mama shouted at me.'

Minna laughed. 'Mama never shouts. What did you say to make her so cross?'

'I told her we should go to Europe for Louis' sake. All of us, to find his grave. The Alstons are going to find Charlie. We should go too.'

Minna cupped her hand around Tiney's chin and tilted her head upwards. 'Darling, that's a mad idea. It would cost a fortune.'

'We could write to Onkel Ludwig and ask him to give us Ma's trust funds.'

'What would we live on when we got back?' asked Minna. 'Mama's trust fund isn't so big, you know. We couldn't manage without it. We certainly can't live on the little bits of money I make teaching, and as much as I love your poems, I've never heard of a rich poet.'

'Perhaps I could be like Jane Eyre and find a position as a governess.'

'Jane Eyre only had to take care of herself. And who would support Ma and Pa when they are old if there is no trust fund? Thea and I can take care of ourselves and Ray will take care of Nette. I'm sure you'd make a very good teacher or governess, Tiney, but you wouldn't earn enough to support anyone except yourself. And if you marry, then you'll have to quit your job. That's the law. And will your husband want to support his new in-laws?'

'No one's ever going to want to marry me,' said Tiney. 'I'm too small and plain and dowdy. You and Thea and Netta and Mama and Papa, you're the only ones that matter to me. If we could go to Europe together it would fix us, it would fix everything.'

'We're not broken,' said Minna. 'And someone will fall in love with you, Tiney. Seventeen is too young to give up on love.'

'You sound just like Nette. But she wouldn't be marrying Ray Staunton so quickly if she wasn't heartbroken about Percy,' said Tiney, sitting down on the end of the bed and folding her arms across her chest.

'I'm not like Nette. I'm not getting married just for the sake of it. If George McCaffrey thinks I'll have him, he's crazier than he looks. I may never get married. And maybe you and Thea won't either. But that doesn't mean we're broken.'

'But without Louis, it's as if there's a big hole in the middle of our family, in the middle of me. My chest hurts all the time, as if my heart's been torn out.'

'Don't, Tiney! If I think too much of Louis, a great black cloud swallows me up.' Minna suddenly looked much older, her whole body limp with grief.

From the back of the house, they heard Nette calling for Tiney. It was time to go and meet the train that was bringing Nette's fiancé, Ray Staunton, home to Adelaide.

'Will you come with us to meet Ray?' asked Tiney.

'No,' said Minna. 'I have students this afternoon and besides, I couldn't bear it. Every soldier that comes home reminds me that Louis never will. But it's important that you go with Nette. She'll need you. You may be our baby sister, but you know we all count on you, Tiney.'

The station was crowded with people, mostly women: sad old ladies, plump mothers and glamorous flappers. Dozens of children darted excitedly up and down the platform. The stationmaster looked exasperated, as platform passes were supposed to be banned because of the flu quarantines. Everyone had been instructed to not throw confetti, in case the soldiers were still suffering shell-shock. Nette and Tiney pushed their way through the throng and stared along the tracks to see if the train was in sight.

Ray's ship had docked at Fremantle weeks before but all the men had been quarantined. When Ray finally got a clean bill of health, he and the other soldiers had to travel by train to reach Adelaide as the ports were closed.

Some men had dozens of family members and they waved welcome banners high. Others, like Ray, had only one or two people waiting for them. Tiney was glad she was there. Ray had no family to celebrate his return.

Three years ago, Ray had proposed to Nette in large scrawly

handwriting looping across crumpled pages. He'd written from the trenches, just before he was about to go 'over the top'.

Minna had tried to stop Nette from accepting. 'You can't marry him!' she'd said. 'You barely know him.'

Nette replied that she could hardly refuse a man when he might be about to die. Percy McCaffrey had been dead a year and Nette wrote her reply without knowing whether Ray had survived the charge.

Tiney remembered the exact moment when Nette had opened Ray's letter announcing that he'd survived the battle and was glad she was promised to him. Nette's expression had been hard to read. She had neither smiled nor wept, but simply folded the pages neatly and tucked them into the pocket of her apron. Then she'd looked up at her parents defiantly and said, 'Ray and I are engaged to be married.'

Now, waiting on the railway platform for Ray, there was a wide-eyed anxiety in Nette's face. 'I don't even know if I'll recognise him,' she whispered.

Nette had dressed carefully in a pale green frock with white batiste at the collar and cuffs, and a new close-fitting cloche hat with a dark green bow on the side. Around her neck she wore a simple necklace with a brown chiastolite stone pendant set in silver. One of the other Cheer-Up girls had told Tiney that chiastolite was good luck. Nette proposed that each sister chip in to buy one of the stones and then they could take turns wearing the pendant, as they couldn't afford to own one each. The sisters agreed it was only right that Nette should wear it for Ray's return but Tiney thought the black cross at the centre of the stone looked onimous rather than lucky.

'It feels like a party, doesn't it?' said Nette, anxiously

smoothing down a strand of fair hair that had escaped from her cloche hat. 'Perhaps we should have simply married on the railway platform!'

'Maybe you should wait,' said Tiney. 'Ray can go ahead and build his house and then you can get married next year, after he's sorted a home for you both.'

'Ray wants to get married straight away. He wants us both to be in Cobdogla by the end of the month. He signed on to the scheme even before he left London.'

'I can't believe you'll leave us so soon,' said Tiney.

Nette put an arm around Tiney's shoulders. 'I know what the others think,' said Nette, touching the chiastolite pendant. 'But Ray is good and kind. I don't care if he's not the brilliant man Pa thinks I should marry. I will help make him whoever he wants to be.'

'But you don't have to do it straight away. You could tell him you're still in mourning for Louis.'

'Tiney, you don't understand. Marrying Ray will bring me one step *closer* to Louis. Through Ray, I can make up for all that we lost when Louis died.'

Tiney couldn't quite see the logic in this line of thinking. She pressed her lips together to stop any contrary words escaping. It came again, that wilful, irrepressible thought, crowding in on her – the longing to drag Nette away, to take the whole family on a ship to Europe.

A shout of welcome went up from the crowd, drowning out the screeching of the train's brakes. Then men began pouring onto the platform, larger than life in their slouch hats and uniforms, their kitbags on their shoulders. Families surged forward to embrace their sons and wives their husbands.

Ray was easy to spot, his craggy face looming above the crowd. His eyes skidded over the Flynns at first but Nette tore off her hat and waved. Her blonde hair shone like a beacon. Ray's face broke into a smile of relief and he shouldered his way towards them.

For a moment, Nette and Ray stood awkwardly staring at each other and then Ray put his arm around Nette and hugged her. Tiney saw that Ray had lost three fingers on his left hand and she looked away, ashamed that she should be thinking of what it would feel like to be caressed by a fingerless man. At least Ray had all the fingers on his right hand, and his thumb and ring finger on the left had been spared, even if they were scarred and twisted. Tiney wondered if he'd choose to wear a wedding ring.

Cod's heads and kerosene lamps

Mama had set out all the ingredients for dinner on the scrubbed timber benchtop. Suet, pork forcemeat, thyme, parsley, lemon rind and juice, and a great big ugly cod's head.

It was Tiney's job to stuff the fishhead. She sat on a stool and jammed a kitchen needle into the cod's leathery skin to sew the stuffed head shut. Cod's head, offal and pigs trotters were among Mama's favourite dishes. Tiney knew it was because they were inexpensive and could stretch to feed the whole family cheaply. Mama made sure they tasted delicious but Tiney longed for roast chicken. Before the war, Papa had taught German at Adelaide High School and in the evening he had tutored private students. Back then, the Flynn family enjoyed roast chicken every Sunday. But when the teaching of German was banned, Papa lost his job. Louis' soldier's pay had helped cover some of the family expenses during the war years but now that had stopped with his death and there was even less to spare.

Thea and Ma sat at the kitchen table, household accounts spread out before them, tallying up columns of figures. Thea took off her glasses and rubbed her eyes. 'Mr Ashton said he'd employ me to take the outdoor painting classes but he doesn't pay very well. I wish the Wilderness School would invite me back to teach painting. A few extra shillings would make such a difference with the wedding expenses.'

Nette's wedding was going to be a simple affair, but everyone in the family was anxious about what to give Nette and Ray for a wedding gift. There were so many extra expenses, not least the food for the guests at the reception. Tiney jabbed the cod's head and prayed that Mama wouldn't put fishheads on the menu.

If it wasn't for Mama's trust fund the Flynn family would never make ends meet. Wolfgang Schomberg, Tiney's grandfather, had been a wealthy man. Mama would never say exactly how much the trust sent each month but Tiney remembered how much better life had been when Opa was still alive. Opa would have understood her plan to go to Europe. He would have helped. She remembered going out to her grandfather's property in the Barossa, and riding beside him in a trap along a dusty country road while he went to visit his patients. On the ride back to his house, he would sing in German and make Tiney sing along. He always spoke German to her, though he was born in Australia and could speak perfect English. And then, back at her grandparents' sprawling Barossa home, the whole family would gather around the table to eat roast pork and steamed potatoes and dumplings and applesauce. But that was before the war, when Opa and Louis and Will had been alive.

Tiney put the stuffed cod's head into the Kooka oven and set potatoes to boil on the stovetop. She scrubbed the fishy smell from her hands with cut lemons and then sat down beside Thea.

'I'm sorry to ask, but I need a new dress,' said Tiney. 'Not just for the wedding. There's the Cheer-Up Victory Ball in July, and once the flu epidemic is over and quarantine restrictions are lifted, there'll be so many dances and I have nothing to wear.'

'But you have a new one,' said Mama. 'I cut down Minna's blue cotton dress for you last month.'

Tiney put her head in her hands and sighed. She didn't want to point out that Minna's old dress was so worn-out it couldn't possibly be thought of as 'new'. All through their childhood, Nette's dresses were cut down for Thea, Thea's for Minna, Minna's for Tiney. Her clothes weren't simply second-hand, they were fourth-hand. Some days Tiney rubbed the fabric of her skirt between her fingers and wondered why the material hadn't grown translucent with wear.

'We will see,' said Mama, as if acknowledging Tiney's despair.

'Ask Minna for ideas,' whispered Thea.

Tiney found Minna in their bedroom, standing in front of the cheval mirror. Minna was trying on her new dress.

'Do you like it?' she asked. 'Is it dainty enough for a "sister of the bride"?'

Mr Timson, a cloth merchant whose daughter was one of Minna's students, had given her a length of deep blue crepe de Chine after his daughter passed her preliminary clarinet exam. Minna had set to work with needle and thread, cutting and stitching. She had folded the fabric over and over in deep pleats and pressed it carefully, then sewn it into a three-tiered tunic that fitted her like a sheath. Beneath the dress she wore a close-fitting white satin shift with full-length mitten sleeves and, for contrast against the dark blue fabric, a long strand of artificial pearls.

The pleats rippled as Minna pirouetted on her toes.

'It's beautiful,' said Tiney, feeling admiration mixed with envy. Minna stopped spinning and rested her hands on Tiney's shoulders. 'There's enough fabric left over for me to make you a blouse.'

'A blouse would be nice, but I need a dress. A dress for the wedding.'

Minna looked at Tiney appraisingly. 'The good thing about making clothes for you is that I don't need a lot of cloth. I could talk to Mr Timson and see if he would give me a few yards of something interesting. But I want to ask you a favour in return. My shoes. They're so drab and ordinary. Do you remember those brooches, the matching diamante ones that Paul gave us for Christmas? Could I swap one of my other brooches for yours? So I'll have a pair of them, you see.'

'Nette says they're too gaudy to wear. You don't have to swap them for anything.'

'But I want to do a swap. And Paul has very good taste, really he does. He just doesn't know about girls, that's all.'

Tiney opened the small wooden box in which she kept her meagre collection of jewellery. The diamante brooch looked loud and ugly sitting beside the tiny cameos and beaded floral brooches. Tiney handed it over and Minna deftly removed the pin. Then she took the two brooches and fixed them to her black day shoes.

'That's so clever, Minna!' Tiney realised that with the large silver and black diamante brooches winking, drawing attention to the slenderness of Minna's ankles, the drab black leather shoes were scarcely noticeable.

'Come here and I'll give you one of my brooches in exchange,' said Minna.

'No, that's all right,' said Tiney. 'I never would have worn the diamantes.'

Minna laughed and opened her jewellery box.

'I know you think things like dreams and spirits aren't to be trusted, but I dreamt about you last night so I know you must have this brooch. Come here and let me pin it on you. When you see it, you'll know why you have to wear it.'

Tiney stepped close to allow Minna to pin the new brooch on her brown cardigan. When she looked down, she smiled. The brooch was in the shape of a boat, with a sharp, slender sail in bright red guilloche enamel arcing like a crescent moon above a small Florentine brass boat.

'I love it,' said Tiney, touching the red sail with her fingertips.

'I knew you would. I dreamt you were in this tiny boat, or at least one with red sails, sailing across a very green ocean.' She hugged Tiney. 'But you won't go away and leave us, will you? Not like Nette.'

'I wish Nette wasn't getting married,' said Tiney.

'Do you dislike Ray so much?' asked Minna, half smiling. In truth, no one really liked Ray, much as they all wanted to admire him.

'It's not about Ray. It's about us. All being together. He's going to take her away and we won't be able to do things the way we used to.'

'There's still you and me and Thea,' said Minna. 'And Victory Balls galore!' She danced a few steps of the Charleston, and the diamante brooches sparkled as she moved. Then she put her arms out and sang, '*You'd better be nice to them now!*'

Tiney giggled and sang along. Minna was right. There were still plenty of reasons to be cheerful, and even if Nette was going away at least they could dance at her wedding.

Tiney felt the hot north wind at her back as she stood on the steps of the church, looking about for somewhere to put her bowl of wilting rose petals. She shouldn't have bothered to bring it. She'd forgotten that Ray, like many soldiers, couldn't bear to have things thrown in his direction. It made him flinch.

Papa was grim-faced as he walked with Nette down the aisle and Mama, sitting in the front pew, wept all through the ceremony. Minna and Thea looked pale. Tiney tried to be happy, for Nette's sake, but she felt it too. Louis' absence. It was as if his shadow fell square and dark across the wedding party. When Ray and Nette made their vows, Tiney squeezed Thea and Minna's hands as if to reassure herself and them of the solidarity of sisters.

Nette had been saying the wedding would give the family something joyful to celebrate together and it was true Minna had gladly made the wedding gown, and Tiney and Thea had sewn tiny artificial seed pearls onto the hem. Ma brought out the lace veil that she'd worn at her own wedding and placed it in Nette's hands. Pa gave Ray a beautifully bound copy of his and Louis' favourite novel, *David Copperfield*, as a way of welcoming him into the family, though they all knew that Ray wasn't really a reader like Louis and Papa. But the wedding reception wasn't a glorious affair. Now that the influenza epidemic had spread across Adelaide, many of the guests were too frightened to attend. Schools were closed, half the city had shut down, fever tents had been pitched in the parks and the Alstons had postponed their Victory Ball.

At the height of summer, the garden at Larksrest couldn't

help but look dull, though at least the wisteria was still in bloom on the front verandah. Tiney and Thea decorated the lychgate with white ribbons, bows and a silver horseshoe. But when they returned from the church, Tiney looked up and saw that the horseshoe had slipped askew and was hanging the wrong way, with the tips pointing downward, as if all the young couple's future happiness would pour away onto the path.

In the front parlour, Tiney, Minna and Thea waited on the wedding party. Ray's only relatives were an uncle and aunt that he didn't seem to know particularly well. Tante Bea and Onkel Ludwig had come down from the Barossa and sat quietly in the front parlour of Larksrest with Paul between them, as if they were being careful to make sure he said nothing to upset Nette on her wedding day. Mama sat with Tante Bea too. Apart from Ida only two of Nette's friends from the Cheer-Ups had braved the quarantines and come along.

When Tiney came back to the parlour with a second tray of cucumber sandwiches, she realised that Papa had left the room. Where was he? Didn't he understand that this could be the last time all his daughters were together under their father's roof?

When she opened the door to his study, she found Papa slumped at the desk, a letter open before him.

'What is it, Pa? You should be with our guests,' said Tiney.

'I am missing your brother today,' said Papa. Tiney saw the official War Office letterhead and felt a flicker of alarm. But it couldn't be bad news. There was no worse news than losing Louis.

'They still don't know where he's buried.' Papa tapped the letter and read out a passage: '*The only information yet available is the brief advice "died of wounds on 18.9.18".*'

All day, every day, Papa sat at his desk, working on his scrapbook of Louis' life or writing letters to find out what had happened to him in his last weeks alive. Papa wrote to the International Red Cross. He wrote to the AIF. He wrote to the Minister for Defence. Always the same six questions: what was the address of Louis' commanding officer, how did he receive his fatal wounds, where was he wounded and how had he died, who were the doctor and nurse in attendance, and where was he buried? He always added, 'Any further particulars?' as if there was one particular detail that might help to make sense of what had happened to his only son.

'They'll send us something more eventually, Papa,' said Tiney. 'Come back to the party, please. It's Nette's day today. She'll be leaving for Cobdolga soon and you must be there when we give her and Ray their wedding gift.'

Papa nodded but he didn't move. Back in the parlour, Tiney discovered that Ray's uncle and aunt had left already, though it was considered bad luck for guests to leave before the bride and groom. Mama beckoned everyone to gather around the table on which the wedding presents had been laid out. There was a set of bone-handled cutlery from Tante Bea and Onkel Ludwig, a rather ordinary-looking teapot from Ray's uncle and aunt, an Irish linen tablecloth from the Alstons; but the biggest gift stood at the back of the table, draped in a red velvet shawl. At a nod from Mama, Minna pulled back the shawl to reveal the gift that Mama had picked out for Nette and Ray. Nette gasped with pleasure. Standing in the centre of the table was a tall, elegant table lamp with an ebonised stand. Knowing that when Nette was living on Ray's soldier-settler land at Cobdolga she would have no gas and no electricity, Mama had searched for the perfect light for her daughter's new home.

Tiney had always thought of kerosene lamps as dull, functional things but this lamp was exquisite, with a shiny black base supporting a brass column, topped by a finely etched crystal shade. Nette cupped her hands around the crystal. 'It's beautiful,' she said.

She glanced at Ray, who was standing near the doorway, looking uncomfortable in his too-tight wedding suit. Ray nodded, as if in agreement, but it was obvious that he was tired of being polite and anxious to leave, to have Nette all to himself. They would spend their wedding night at Tailem Bend, breaking the fourteen-hour trip to Renmark. Then they would begin their married life in a boarding house while Ray built a home for them on the land the government had granted him in the Riverina district near the Murray River. For a moment, Tiney hated him. He didn't feel like a member of their family. He was a thief, come to steal Nette away from everyone who loved her.

Ray lumbered across the room, looking first at the lamp and then at Nette. Tiney wanted him to say something romantic, something about Nette being the light of his life, anything that would show that he understood how lucky he was to have her. Ray touched the crystal shade with the gnarled finger of his damaged hand and said, 'That'll be a bugger to get to Cobdolga without breaking it.'

Voices of the dead

On a hot afternoon in late March, Tiney and Minna stepped off the Goodwood tram. A gritty north wind made them shield their eyes.

'I'm glad you're with me,' said Minna, consulting the piece of paper with the address on it. 'Tilda said I had to bring someone with me so that there was no risk of there being five people at the table.'

'What's wrong with having five?' asked Tiney.

'Tilda says that Christ was murdered with five wounds. There are five sides to a pentagon and five points on a pentacle, and so five can bring sinister forces into the room.'

'So I'm only here to help out Tilda?'

'We're lucky Tilda said we could come along at all. Mrs Constance-Higgens normally holds her meetings in public halls and charges admission, but these sessions are private and they're free. Tilda asked us especially. She said this séance is only for direct communication with people who have lost family.'

'I don't know that I want to talk to Louis. At least, not like this.'

'Not like this? Do you mean you have other ways of talking to him?'

Tiney looked at the tip of her shoes and wished she hadn't come. 'I don't think Mama would approve of talking to him like this,' she said obstinately.

Minna ignored her. 'Tilda's house is over there,' she said, pointing to a red-brick house behind a high hedge.

Inside the gate, pointy conifers lined the path to the door and added a funereal pall to the entrance.

Tilda opened the door. Tall and thin, with eyes too big for her face, she unnerved Tiney. 'You're late,' she said, looking anxious. 'Everyone else is here.'

She led them into a gloomy sitting room off a long central hallway. 'Everyone else' turned out to be six other visitors. Tilda introduced Tiney and Minna to the group. There was an elderly couple, a soldier in uniform with a girl who seemed to be his sister, a stout old gentleman, and a young woman who looked so pale she might have already seen a ghost. Tiney felt sorry for her, coming alone to the séance.

'Mother is preparing herself,' said Tilda.

Tiney took a seat beside the old gentleman, who introduced himself as Captain Oliphant.

'Nothing to worry about, little ladies,' he said, as if sensing their nervousness. 'The spirit entities will speak for themselves through using the brain and vocal organs of our medium. But remember that even though the dead are speaking through her, they can't hurt you.'

Mrs Constance-Higgens entered the room so quietly that it seemed she might have been waiting in the shadows of the hall watching the guests arrive. Tiney had imagined she would have an imposing presence but she was reed-like, with hollowed-out cheeks and hands like bird's claws. Without speaking, she sat at the head of the table, her eyes averted. Tilda sat on a stool to one side, shorthand notebook and pen at the ready.

'Mother has been preparing herself to speak with the spirit entities,' said Tilda. 'She must sink deeply into a trance to allow the spirits to enter her. She submits to the control of the spirits for your sakes. Because she believes it is your right to speak to your loved ones.'

The young woman let out a small moan and Captain Oliphant patted her shoulder comfortingly.

'You must all join hands,' said Tilda. 'Do not let go of your neighbour's hand, or the chain will be broken.'

The curtains were drawn, blocking out the afternoon sun. The room felt stuffy and close. A candle on the mantelpiece glowed blue and Tiney shivered despite the heat.

The first voice that came from Mrs Constance-Higgens was deep and rich. It was extraordinary to hear a man's voice emanating from this thin, pale woman.

'I am the Healing Master,' the voice said. 'My dear friend Angelica gives me a vessel through which I can share with you. I come to speak of the world of the spirit, to reassure you that you will find peace when you cross over to join us.'

Tiney felt Minna's hand grip hers tighter and she squeezed back.

Then Mrs Constance-Higgen's head tipped back and she made a gurgling sound in her throat. When she spoke again, it was in a completely different voice, in a language that no one understood.

'Is that you, Chief?' asked Tilda.

'Oginali,' said Mrs Constance-Higgens. 'Otsalanvlvi.'

'What is she saying?' asked the soldier.

'The Chief is welcoming us as his friends. He says we are all brothers and sisters,' said Captain Oliphant.

'What language is that?' asked Tiney.

'Cherokee Indian. From America,' whispered Captain Oliphant.

Mrs Constance-Higgens groaned, and Tilda spoke sharply to Tiney. 'Please do not converse while the spirits are manifesting unless given permission to do so.'

Mrs Constance-Higgens tossed her head from side to side as if in pain and then a third voice came from her. This time, though still using a man's voice, the spirit spoke in English. Not only in English but in rhyme, with a smooth, elegant British accent.

And "art is long", and "life is short",
And man is slow at learning;
And yet by divers dealings taught,
For divers follies yearning,
He owns at last, with grief downcast
(For man disposed to grieve is) –
One adage old stands true and fast,
"Ars longa, vita brevis."'

'I know that poem,' said Tiney. 'That's by Adam Lindsay Gordon.'

'Shhh!' said Tilda irritably.

The voice continued.

'I am the poet you know well,
Now in a realm of ether
I come with many truths to tell

Death my noble teacher
Your lads that fought so brave and strong
Now rest as heroes near me
This night they'll speak to you ere long
And share their secrets with thee.'

'He definitely didn't write that bit,' said Tiney in an undertone. Minna squeezed her hand so hard that she winced.

The medium began to moan again and Tilda spoke. 'Mother feels there are negative vibrations in the room. Unbelievers will deter the spirits from entering her.'

'No, we all believe,' cried the old woman to Tiney's left, leaning forward. 'Don't let our boys be deterred by a chit of a girl.' She glared at Tiney.

Mrs Constance-Higgens began to cough and gag and writhe. Her cheeks billowed out and something began to emerge from her mouth. The soldier's sister let out a shriek and tried to draw away from the table.

'Don't let go of each other's hands!' cried Tilda. 'You must hold fast. Don't be afraid.'

'What's happening?' whimpered the soldier's sister.

'I don't like this,' said the soldier.

'It's all right, young chap,' said Captain Oliphant. 'It's ectoplasm – the spirit made flesh – a manifestation from the other side.'

The medium coughed and coughed until she disgorged a wad of stringy substance, flecked with bits of blood. Tiney watched in disgust as a second long, flesh-white lump coated in saliva began to ooze out of Mrs Constance–Higgens' mouth onto the black velvet tablecloth. Everyone stared. Tiney let go of Captain Oliphant's hand and reached out to touch it.

'Don't!' shrieked Tilda. 'Touching ectoplasm is dangerous – you could kill my mother. On the ectoplasm will appear the image of the first spirit who will speak tonight. Spirit, name yourself!'

Captain Oliphant reached for Tiney's hand again and held it tightly. Then the air seemed to shimmer around them. One of the young women peered closely at the white lump in horror. 'It's Alan. I can see his face. My Alan. Oh my God,' she said, breaking into sobs. 'Alan, Alan, are you there?'

The voice that came out of the medium was soft and deep. 'Elsie, my Elsie.'

'Yes, I'm here,' said Elsie, leaning across the table as if she might kiss Mrs Constance-Higgens.

'You're wearing my ring, Elsie. But I don't hold you to your promise. I want you to go to the ball and dance all night, as we did. Those boys who come back, they need you, Elsie. I'm at peace. At peace.'

'Alan, is Percy McCaffrey with you?' asked Minna.

Elsie looked at Minna with a hurt expression. Then she turned to Mrs Constance-Higgens. 'Don't leave, Alan, don't go yet,' she cried.

'Minna?' came a different voice. 'Why do you seek me and not your brother Louis?'

Minna gasped. 'Percy, we miss you too, Percy.' Silvery tears were coursing down her face.

'It's George that's for you. Let me go, Minna.'

Tiney stared at her sister. 'Minna?' she whispered. She longed for the séance be over, for them both to be out of the hot, dark room. She shut her eyes, felt a trickle of sweat down the back of her neck.

Mrs Constance-Higgens began to hum and then the humming turned into words. 'Minna, Martina, little Tiney,' she said, again in a man's voice. 'Why do you seek Percy McCaffrey instead of me, your own brother?'

Tiney felt a little prick of irritation. Louis had never called her Martina and hardly ever Tiney. She was always his 'Titch'.

'Do you want to ask Louis a question, Tiney?' said Tilda, gently. 'He won't stay with Mother for long. There are hundreds, thousands of soldiers seeking a voice through her.'

Tiney shook her head. She didn't want to hear another word emanate through the lips of Mrs Constance-Higgens. But as she tried to slip her hand out of Captain Oliphant's again, the table began to twitch. It rose up inches from the floor and shook. The little mound of ectoplasm wobbled and Elsie and Minna began to weep hysterically.

'Stay calm,' said Captain Oliphant. 'It's these girls' brother sending them a sign, that's all.'

Tiney sank back into her seat, wishing she could disappear.

The rest of the séance seemed interminably long as more dead soldiers spoke through the medium. The elderly couple had lost three of their sons and each one sent a brief, cryptic message from the grave. Captain Oliphant's nephew spoke too.

Finally, the voice of the Healing Master returned. He sounded both wearier and more pompous than he had at the beginning of the evening. As he finished speaking, Mrs Constance-Higgens began to swoon. Suddenly, she fell forward across the table, her hair coming loose and spreading like cobwebs across the black velvet. Tilda quickly scooped the pile of ectoplasm into a bowl and then she and Captain Oliphant helped Mrs Constance-Higgens to her feet and led her from the room. The séance was over.

The guests sat in stunned silence. The grieving old mother wept silently, tears dripping from her chin into her lap. Her husband studied his hands. The soldier took out a silver cigarette case and lit up.

When Tilda returned she said, 'Mother is too exhausted to come out. There was so much pressure from the other side, too many men seeking communion with us. I'm afraid it will take her days to recover. However, she whispered that she was glad to be of service to you all and hopes you found some solace. She asks nothing of you but that you think of her kindly. She will be giving a public trance on Saturday evening at the drill hall, for which she'll charge a small fee. This séance was a gift to you all, but if you do wish to repay Mother's kindness you may leave something in the crystal bowl on the mantelpiece.'

Captain Oliphant was first to place a thick roll of notes into the bowl. The elderly couple whispered to each other and then the old man followed suit. Tiney thought they must have put in forty pounds between them. One by one, the guests put coins and pound notes into the bowl. Elsie even took off one of her rings and dropped it in among the cash. Tiney felt uneasy, as if everyone was watching them, especially Captain Oliphant. Then Minna reached into her bag and pulled out her cloth purse.

'What are you doing?' whispered Tiney. 'You're not going to give them any money, are you? It wasn't Louis, you know it wasn't him.'

Minna frowned. 'But that was Percy. I'm sure it was. And what if we just can't remember what Louis' voice sounds like any more? It's been over four years.'

Tiney rolled her eyes. Before she could stop her, Minna had slipped a whole pound note into the crystal bowl on the mantelpiece.

In the street, the two girls walked swiftly to the tram stop. Tiney wanted to run. It was such a relief to be out in the open again and she could barely suppress her fury.

Minna stared out the window as the tram rattled back across town. Tiney wanted to shake her. 'That was awful. Why did you want to talk to Percy?' she asked.

'Why do you think? It was Percy that I loved. Now I'm meant to like George, as if one brother is as good as another.'

'Percy? You never said a word about loving Percy! You were only sixteen when he went to war. But you do like George, just a little, don't you? He was always the handsome one,' said Tiney.

Minna pursed her lips and stared at her little sister. 'George is mad. Whether it was the mustard gas or the whisky, he's not right. But I'm not allowed to say it out loud. I'm meant to pretend that I like him when I don't.'

She turned to Tiney, grasping both her hands. 'Did you read about that girl down in Port Pirie who broke off with her fiancé when he came back?'

'You mean the one who died?'

'Tiney, she didn't die. Her fiancé shot her. He murdered her and then he turned the gun on himself.'

'Maybe it was an accident,' said Tiney, desperate to make sense of the tragedy.

'It wasn't an accident. And it's happened to other girls.'

'I know it's ghastly, but surely you're not afraid that George would do that, are you?'

'Probably not. George seems more broken than twisted. But

who can know anyone now? The war has turned those boys inside out, and the skins they're wearing, they're not the skins they left home in.'

'But Minna, we have to remember what they went through, always.'

Minna sighed and cupped her hands around her chin. 'No one had a kind word to say about that dead girl from Port Pirie. They all thought she was awful and a coward for not going through with marrying her soldier. Tilda said she deserved to die. But does anyone deserve a life of misery with a man they don't love, just because he fought in the war?'

'You don't have to marry George,' said Tiney.

'He hasn't asked – yet,' said Minna, worrying the edge of her sleeve, plucking at the frayed edge.

'If he does ask, you can say no,' said Tiney. 'Just because Nette got married, it doesn't mean you have to as well.'

'Sometimes I feel I have to marry someone and yet there's hardly anyone left,' said Minna, staring gloomily out the window at the darkened street. Tiney followed her gaze. She understood how Minna felt – they were pitching forward into an uncertain future.

Hope tests its wings

'If I have to wear this stupid mask for another month longer, I'll lose my mind,' said Ida Alston as she pulled off her wimple and face-mask and flung them onto the table in the little kitchen of the Cheer-Up Hut. 'We can't go on acting as if the world is coming to an end because of that ruddy Spanish influenza.'

'It does feel as though the quarantine is going to last forever,' said Tiney, sweeping carrot peelings into the bin. 'The newspaper said there are more than two hundred people in hospital and they still haven't opened the schools. I was thinking of applying for a position as a teacher's aide or sitting the examination but I don't even know when they're going to set the exams for admission to the College.'

'It's not stopping everyone from celebrating. The Victory Ball at the Town Hall is going ahead in July. Even the Refused Volunteers Society is holding a Masque ball next month. You know they've asked for the Cheer-Ups to help with refreshments.'

Tiney let out a small groan. 'I always seem to be serving at parties. I never get to dance or have any fun. You know, Ida, I don't think I can go on being a Cheer-Up much longer. It's not the same without Nette and I just don't feel cheerful enough any more.'

Ida quietly shut the door that opened onto the main kitchen, pulled up a bentwood chair, and kicked off her shoes.

'I know exactly what you mean. I'm feeling ragged myself.' She lifted one of her feet onto her lap and began rubbing her ankle. 'I shouldn't complain in front of you, kid. I've done more than my fair share of dancing. It's such a silly rule not to allow girls under eighteen to join the fun. But don't worry. You can come to our party and dance all night if you like.'

'I thought you'd cancelled because your mother was worried about the epidemic?'

'She's almost as fed up as me. Besides, they say the restrictions will be eased at the end of the month. And there are boys coming home in droves. We have to welcome them. If Charlie was one of them we would have thrown a ball the minute he stepped off the ship, influenza be damned.'

'But they've stopped the interstate trains and they're even going to stop the HMS *Australia* from landing.'

'Pooh. That won't stop us. There are thousands who've come home already. Mother has said we should go ahead regardless. We're going to host a proper masquerade ball, the sort the Society of Arts should be organising. We're going to beat those Refused Volunteers to the punch and throw the most gorgeous fancy-dress extravaganza imaginable.'

Tiney had never realised what a tonic the idea of a party could be. For two weeks, the Flynn sisters talked about nothing but the

Alstons' ball. Even Mama put down her embroidery and helped with their costumes. Minna had made a special arrangement with Mr Timson, the cloth merchant, providing extra lessons for his daughter in exchange for lengths of cloth, and now the sisters were busy designing their own outfits. Even Thea was excited. So often, Thea politely declined invitations to parties and retreated to her studio. But from the moment the Alstons' invitation arrived, she'd begun counting the days until the masque ball.

It was Thea's idea that they should all go as Commedia dell'Arte characters, Harlequin, Pierrot and Columbine. She found a beautiful postcard of the trio and set it upon the dresser in her bedroom for inspiration.

Minna sewed pink and black diamond-shaped pieces of material together to make Harlequin fabric for herself. Tiney was to go as Pierrot and Thea as Columbine.

They made their fancy-dress masks from cardboard and plaster of Paris and Thea painted these carefully to match their outfits. Mama lent her 'special' sewing box, filled with tiny beads, coloured threads and feathers. She even showed Tiney how to make black pompoms to sew onto her Pierrot outfit.

On the evening of the ball, Tiney stood before the mirror admiring her silky-smooth white costume. Minna had helped her make white ruffs for the collar, sleeves and ankles and sewn a few artfully placed black circles on the shining satin. Tiney gathered up her long blonde hair and tucked it under a black skullcap. With her face painted white, her lips a small red bow and her features carefully highlighted in black, she looked like a perfect Parisian Pierrot.

Minna had surprised them by coming home with her hair cut

into a sleek bob. Mama gasped in horror but Tiney and Thea clapped their hands in admiration. On the night of the party, Minna trained a dark lock on her forehead into a kiss curl. She wore a full black skirt and black leggings topped by an elaborate sleeveless blouse fashioned from the Harlequin fabric. A luxurious pink-and-black checked turban with a long swathe of fabric was draped like a scarf across her shoulder.

Thea was annoyingly secretive about her Columbine outfit and was still sewing rosettes onto the skirt when Thea and Tiney were ready to leave.

'You go ahead,' she said, waving them towards the door.

'We can't go without you,' said Tiney.

'Papa will walk me to the party when he takes his evening stroll. Don't worry, I won't be far behind you.'

Tiney and Minna set out to walk the few blocks to the Alstons. The evening was unusually warm for May and Tiney wasn't surprised when Minna stopped and took off her coat. But then Minna hung it over a fence and proceeded to take off her skirt.

'What are you doing?' asked Tiney.

'Mama would have scolded me if I'd left the house without an underskirt but I designed the blouse to work as a skirt. It's much more stylish without all those layers of fabric.'

Minna stripped off and stuffed the black skirt into her raffia basket, then adjusted the folds of the pink-and-black diamond blouse so its pocket-handkerchief hem reached just above her knees. The carefully draped folds of fabric made Minna look svelte and stylish.

'Is it too risqué?' asked Minna, suddenly less brazen.

Tiney paused. 'You look like a French postcard, like a flapper crossed with someone from the Moulin Rouge.'

Minna laughed and struck a pose, her hand on her hip, the raffia basket swinging wide. Then she dropped the basket and put one hand on Tiney's shoulder.

'You won't tell, will you?'

'Some matron will spread rumours about you, but you know I won't.'

Minna had a new shimmy to her walk once she'd rid herself of her skirt. When they reached the gates of the Alstons' mansion, she took their masks from the raffia basket.

'Here, let me adjust yours for you and then you can do mine,' said Minna.

Tiney's was a simple, close-fitting black mask decorated with jet-black beads and white sequins to mirror her black-and-white costume. Minna's mask was pink and black with sharp, winged sides and a V between the eyes that highlighted her perfectly slicked-down kiss-curl. They walked up the Alstons' gravel driveway hand-in-hand, a small Pierrot in glowing white and a glamorous Harlequin.

Ida opened the door. A rush of disinfectant made Tiney's eyes prick with tears but it was Ida's costume that made her blink. Ida was swathed in pale green fabric and wore a crown of flowers and vines in her curly auburn hair.

'Are you a fairy?' asked Tiney.

'Titania, Queen of the Night,' said Ida. She flung her arms in the air and spun about so they could admire her from all angles. A huge pair of gossamer wings were fixed to the back of her gown, and her silver mask was covered with small diamantes.

Then Ida took in what Minna was wearing.

'Is that really Minna Flynn or some flapper from America?'

Did Minna blush? Tiney realised it was hard to tell what anyone was thinking between their masks, makeup and costumes. On a hallstand behind Ida, dozens of masks were laid out for guests who arrived without one.

The Alstons had a small but elegant ballroom with doors that opened onto a side terrace. The terrace was lit with acetylene gas lamps and crowds of soldiers, some in uniform, some in costumes but all in masks, stood beneath the golden glow, smoking. More gas lamps were positioned in the ballroom for when the electricity was cut off at ten o'clock. Ida had said that not even coal shortages could stop her party, once she'd made up her mind it must go ahead.

Every doorway was decorated like a victory arch with the name of a famous battle: Passchendaele, Bullecourt, Fromelles, Pozières, Gallipoli, Villers-Bretonneux. Minna and Tiney found it hard to decide which battle they should stand under. Tiney felt suddenly shy and childish. So many of the other guests were dressed as princess and fairies that her demure Pierrot seemed too boyish.

Every time a new man entered the room, Minna's eyes would flick over him. It was only for a moment and her face gave nothing away, but Tiney had the feeling Minna was waiting and watching for someone, someone in particular.

Then she stiffened and turned her body, bending towards Tiney.

'Talk to me,' hissed Minna. 'Talk to me as if we're having a very interesting conversation.'

'About what?' asked Tiney.

'About anything. Just frown a lot too, as if it's very serious and extremely private. George McCaffrey just came in.'

'He couldn't possibly recognise you, especially not from behind.'

'You don't know George. He'll study every woman in the room until he's found me,' said Minna, her voice tinged with despair.

Tiney tried to help Minna out, talking about how awful the punch tasted and furrowing her brow, but it didn't work.

George tapped Minna on the shoulder. He wasn't in costume but in ordinary civilian clothes. He hadn't even bothered to pick up one of the masks in the hallway.

Minna shut her eyes momentarily, took a breath and turned to face him.

'Oh, hello,' she said. 'I'd imagined you wouldn't recognise me.'

'You filled your dance card?' he asked. His voice sounded odd, and Tiney could smell the bitterness of ale on his breath.

'I haven't filled mine up,' said Tiney. 'I haven't pencilled anyone in yet.'

'I didn't ask you,' said George. Tiney felt hot with embarrassment.

'Mine's full,' said Minna, not batting an eyelid, though Tiney knew she hadn't a single name on it.

'Let me see,' said George, putting out his hand.

'No,' said Minna, pressing the card to her chest.

George grabbed her elbow and twisted her arm towards him in one quick movement, reaching to pluck the card from her hand. Minna let out a gasp of anger.

'Is there a problem, ladies?' A tall, elegant man dressed in black feathers appeared beside Tiney. He was startlingly costumed with a pair of huge black wings on his back and a crow's head and beak perched on his head. Hundreds of ebony feathers shimmered on his close-fitting black leotard. He lifted off his mask and smiled at them with intense brown eyes from beneath a thick mop of blond hair.

George stared hard at the stranger.

'We know each other, don't we?' said the stranger. 'You were at Ypres, Menin Road? I was with the Twenty-seventh Battalion, Second Division.'

George didn't reply. He turned away from them and pushed his way into the crowd.

'So rude,' said Minna, rubbing her arm where George had grabbed it.

The stranger stared after George's disappearing back. 'I don't think he remembers much of anything,' he said before turning to Tiney. 'I'm sorry, ladies. I should have introduced myself. I'm Sebastian Farr. You must be Dorothea's sisters.'

'How do you know our Thea?' asked Minna.

'I've been admiring her work at the Society of Artists. Is she here yet?' asked Sebastian.

'She should be, any minute,' said Minna, glancing around the ballroom. 'She doesn't usually like to come to dances but she made an exception for tonight.'

'I hope she's hiding a secret love of dancing that she's kept from her sisters. I intend to dance with her all night. '

Minna looked thunderstruck and Tiney let out a shout of laughter.

'You must be Martina,' said Sebastian. 'Thea said you were the cheekiest of her sisters. Would you do me the honour of the first dance?'

Tiney blushed. 'You should dance with Minna, she's a much

better dancer than me. Besides, you're so terribly tall and I'm so short, we'll look very odd on the dance floor.'

Sebastian turned to Minna. 'Shall we?'

Minna glanced over her shoulder, frowning at Tiney, as she followed Sebastian onto the dance floor. Had Tiney committed a terrible faux pas? What if Sebastian decided he liked Minna more than Thea? How could he not like Minna more? She was so beautiful. Then Tiney saw Thea passing under the archway of Fromelles. Her costume of apricot silk and tiny pink rosebuds shimmered in the gaslight. Her hair hung loose and curling around her shoulders. Tiney had never seen Thea look so softly feminine. When the song came to its end, Minna and Sebastian crossed the floor to Thea and the three of them stood together, the handsomest trio in the ballroom.

Tiney felt a stab of self-pity. She had probably passed up her only invitation to dance for the evening. Sebastian wouldn't ask her again as he'd be too busy with Thea. Minna would quickly find another dance partner. Tiney would be doomed to spend the evening as a wallflower. She almost wished she was in her Cheer-Up uniform, ladling out glasses of punch. Anything was better than standing alone in her Pierrot costume while the party whirled by.

Then she saw Frank McCaffrey looking miserable in an ill-fitting costume as he stood beneath the Pozières archway. Tiney skirted around the edge of the dance floor to join him.

'Frank, you look dashing. But who are you meant to be?' asked Tiney.

'Aramis, you know, one of the Three Musketeers,' he said, uncomfortably adjusting the floppy feather in his broad-brimmed hat. 'I'm not sold on this masque ball idea. Is this the Alstons' going-away party, or our welcome home? I'd heard they're off to Europe.'

'They are going – eventually,' said Tiney. 'But between the flu and the Germans refusing to sign the treaty, everything's on hold.'

'The Germans would be mad to sign.'

'So you don't agree with Mr Hughes?' asked Tiney.

Frank lowered his voice. 'He made a lot of noise over there at the Paris Peace Conference but he's not doing us a lot of good. He should come home and sort things here. Let Europe clean up her own mess. We've done enough for her. We need to get on with our lives. There are a lot of men that need help and they're arriving by the shipload.'

'There's the soldier-settler scheme. Ray got land without any trouble.'

Frank frowned. 'I hope Ray and Nette took a good look at it before they signed up.'

Tiney thought of the uneasy tone in Nette's letters, the thinly veiled anxiety about their future in the Riverina. She didn't want to tell Frank that Nette and Ray were living in a tent. It made her heart clutch with anxiety.

'I've been lucky,' said Frank. 'I've got a job as a clerk at a good law firm, and I'm studying too. Not like poor George.'

Tiney felt her heart sink. Now they would have to discuss George and how the war had broken him and then Tiney would start to feel guilty on Minna's behalf, because Minna could never love George. Tiney saw the evening stretch out before her, a long night of thinking about her sisters and worrying about the state of the world. Then she realised she was being rude, not responding to Frank's conversation.

'I'm sorry, Frank. Did you just ask me a question?'

Frank smiled. 'Martina Flynn,' said Frank. 'Would you mind dancing with a digger – or a musketeer – with two left feet?'

'You want to dance?' asked Tiney. 'With me?'

Frank took hold of Tiney's hands and led her onto the dance floor. They spun out onto the smooth marble as the band struck up a foxtrot. Tiney looked up into Frank's face. The lights glanced off his glasses, making his eyes appear an even deeper blue.

Sebastian and Thea passed by as Frank guided Tiney through the crowd of dancers. Minna, dancing with a new partner, smiled and waved. It was a long time since Tiney had seen such an expression of easy happiness on Minna's face. But then Tiney turned her gaze back to Frank. Frank and Tiney. Tiney and Frank. She liked the way their names sounded, sitting side by side. For the first time in months, Tiney felt a flutter of hope, like a small bird testing its wings, move inside her.

12

Lost and found

Tiney racked her brain, trying to think what was the last thing that Minna said before she disappeared. Had they argued? Had Tiney spoken sharply? Was there something she said that tipped Minna over the edge? Or was one of the men Minna had danced with connected to her disappearance?

The morning after the Alstons' ball, Tiney had been slow to wake up. By the time she did, Minna was gone. Her bed was neatly made, the coverlet smooth, the pillow plumped.

Tiney was sitting at the breakfast table, rubbing sleep from her eyes, when Mama came silently into the room and handed her a note. It was on the soft mauve writing paper that Minna used for all her correspondence.

Dearest Mama,

I do not mean to cause you any grief but I have to go away for some time. I can't say when I will be home but events have arisen that have made it clear to me I cannot stay in Adelaide for the moment. I will write again when I am safely settled. Please don't worry about me. I am with friends and in no moral jeopardy.

Your loving daughter, Wilhemina (Minna)

Tiney read it three times, as if the words were incomprehensible. 'Where did you find this?'

'Minna left it propped beside my teacup. It was waiting for me this morning. She must have slipped out before dawn.'

Tiney leapt up from the table and ran back to the bedroom she shared with Minna, searching for some sign of her sister's plans. There was no evidence of a hurried departure, only of a frighteningly clear-headed intent.

The small grey cardboard suitcase that Minna kept under her bed for visits to the country was missing. Some of her wardrobe remained but the blue crepe-de-Chine frock, a black opera cloak and her black silk concert skirt were no longer hanging in the wardrobe. Wherever Minna had gone, she would look her best.

Thea was as bewildered as Tiney by Minna's sudden departure. Papa showed a flash of rage and then retreated to his study, back to the interminable task of building his scrapbook of Louis' life.

'We must make a plan,' said Tiney. 'A plan to find her.'

'What if she doesn't want to be found?' asked Thea.

Tiney ignored Thea's question. 'Let's make a list of all the people who might know something. That ghastly Tilda Constance-Higgens probably has something to do with it. If she doesn't have any answers, then we'll question all Minna's students. And the police, we should call the police too. And Ida – she might have noticed something at last night's ball. Minna danced with a dark-haired man I didn't recognise. He might know something. Or that Sebastian Farr.'

Thea put her hand on Tiney's forearm. 'Mr Farr wouldn't know anything about it. He only danced with her once. And Minna would have danced with every man at the party. You can't go questioning all of them. They'll get the wrong idea about her.'

'Thea's right,' said Mama. 'You must speak to no one about this. If anyone asks, we'll tell them Minna's gone to stay with relatives in the country. We must give her the chance to come back of her own volition, without a scandal.'

'But someone might know where she is! I'm sure Tilda will know something.'

'Minna is a sensible girl. She wouldn't be swayed by someone like Tilda. I trust her to do the right thing,' said Mama. 'Your father and I are very upset, but we have decided the best course of action is to wait. We must all bide our time and give Minna the chance to come home without a fuss.'

Tiney felt her face grow hot, her mouth burn with all the secrets she was keeping from her mother. She thought of Minna kissing the soldier on Armistice Day, of the way men looked at her when they were out together, of Minna peeling off her black skirt and of her spinning across the Alstons' dance floor. Minna was too dangerously beautiful. Couldn't Mama and Thea understand that?

Tiney sat hunched over her morning tea, listening as Mama telephoned every one of Minna's students to explain that Minna wouldn't be taking classes for the next week or two. She felt a sick, hollow feeling in the pit of her stomach. What would they do without Minna's wages? She had been counting on Minna's help in saving up for the trip to Europe. She had been counting on Minna being at Larksrest forever.

By the beginning of June, there was still no word from Minna. At night, the quiet of their bedroom was almost unbearable. Tiney would wake in fright and then realise that it was the silence that woke her. To not hear Minna's gentle breathing made Tiney feel as though she was sleeping in a tomb. A week after Minna had left, Tiney moved her things in with Thea.

Tiney couldn't bear to go to the Cheer-Up Hut any more. She lost interest in the plans for their Victory Ball. Most evenings, after clearing up the kitchen, she would sit quietly in her room and write in her journal or lose herself in a book.

Then, on a bright, clear winter morning, four letters arrived from Nette. Nette wrote twice a week without fail but they'd never all received letters from her at exactly the same time. Papa came to the breakfast table and handed Thea, Tiney and Mama a letter each. As if Minna had only gone out for a walk, he put her letter on the mantelpiece for when she returned. They each took turns using the bone-handled letter-opener to slice open their envelopes.

Tiney read the opening sentence of her letter and clapped one hand over her mouth with surprise. 'Does yours say the same thing as mine?' she asked Thea.

Thea glanced at Mama and Papa, who were both smiling. 'Of course it does. Congratulations, Auntie Tiney!'

Tiney scanned her letter again. 'Does yours say when the baby is due?'

'November,' said Mama. 'Our Nette will become a mother in November.'

'She'll have to come and have the baby in Adelaide,' said Tiney. 'We'll be able to have her home again for months.'

'That will be up to Ray,' said Papa. 'He may want Nette and his child to be with him.'

'He can't!' said Tiney. 'They're still living in a tent!'

'Perhaps this will give him the impetus to finish building the house,' said Mama.

Tiney and Thea looked at each other sceptically but said nothing. Mama and Papa had enough grief and worry to deal with without adding criticism of Ray to their burden.

Tiney was humming cheerfully to herself as she polished the mirror on the hallstand when a courier arrived later in the day. She opened the front door and called for Papa to come and sign the delivery receipt. The parcel was from the Australian Imperial Force. But the courier announced the parcel was addressed to Mama – Mrs Charlotte Flynn. Papa watched carefully as Mama signed.

'Find your sister,' said Papa to Tiney. 'We must open this all together. These are your brother's possessions sent from France.'

In the parlour, Mama laid the parcel on the cedar table and the family sat in a circle as she cut the strings.

The first thing that she took out was a small pouch. She pressed it against her face and smelt the fabric, as if it might still hold the scent of Louis. Then she laid it back down on the brown paper and gently touched the rest of the contents with the tips of her fingers.

'Five years of his life,' she said. 'So little for five years.'

Tiney picked up one of the photos. It was of all four sisters. Louis had carried a picture of them to the trenches. She blinked back tears.

Papa opened up one of the accompanying letters. It was an inventory of Louis' effects.

'The diary, discs, photos, pouch, purse, pipe-lighter, watch chain and his medals and medal ribbons were with him at the front,' he said. 'It says they were "received from the field". The second set of things is from his kitbag held in store.'

Thea took the letter from Papa, looked at it, and then began separating the items into two piles: the ones that were with him when he died and the ones that had been in his kitbag. She glanced at Tiney and smiled as she picked up three pairs of socks. They were ones that each of his sisters had knitted for him. Only the socks that Minna had knitted were missing. Tiney wished Minna was there with them at that moment. To know that her socks were the ones he wore on his last day.

In the pile of things from his kitbag there was a gift tin that Mama had sent him, his unit colours, some badges, a small stack of letters and a single photo of a woman with long dark hair holding a tiny baby. Thea handed the photo to Papa, who in turn handed it to Mama. She studied it closely. 'Who could this be?'

They were all thinking the same thought at the same time, but no one seemed to want to say it out loud.

'Does the baby look like Louis?' asked Tiney.

Thea put one hand up, as if to admonish her sister. 'Louis would have told us if he had married.'

'I would know,' said Mama. 'I would know in my heart if Louis did such a thing.'

Tiney didn't want to remind Mama that she hadn't known that Nette was pregnant for three months before she wrote, or that Minna had been planning to run away until they found her note. When Tiney was little, she'd imagined Mama and Papa knew every thought inside her head. Now, she knew how fallible they were.

Papa snatched the photo from Mama's hands. 'You mustn't jump to wild conclusions. This woman could be anyone. Someone he helped, the wife of one of his comrades. If she meant something to him, he would have carried the photo into battle. But it was among his things in the kitbag.' He turned the photo over. 'There's a date in pencil, here on the back: *May 1915*. Our Louis was in hospital in Malta in May of that year. He would have written to tell me if she were anyone important.'

As if that meant there was to be no more discussion, Papa gathered up the letters from the parcel and Louis' diary and retreated to his study.

Tiney couldn't understand why he and Mama should want to dismiss the possibility that the photo might be of someone important to Louis. She went to her room and drew out her writing folio. Inside was a letter from the Thomas Cook Agency about their tours of the battlefields, costings of travel to England and France, and a letter from the Prime Minister's office saying there would be no assistance for families of the bereaved to visit the battlefields of Europe. Then she drew out a fresh sheet of paper and began to write a letter to Nette congratulating her on the news of the baby and telling her of the arrival of Louis' possessions. As she wrote a description of the photo of the mysterious woman and baby, she lifted her pen and gazed out the window. Was it possible that they were already both aunts?

13

Christie's Beach

The dark had come down early and a wintry night had settled on Larksrest. When Thea reached for her hat and coat from the hallstand, Tiney asked in a whisper, 'Can I come too? Please?'

Thea looked puzzled. 'You want to come to the life drawing class at the Society?'

Tiney blushed. 'I thought it was a lecture. You said there was something about Normandy. Mrs Colbert talking about her trip to paint the ruins. I thought I could ask her about France and...'

Thea touched Tiney's cheek. 'Darling, not your mad plan about France again.'

'Please let me come.' Tiney glanced down the hallway anxiously.

'What's wrong?'

'I can't bear another evening here alone.'

'Mama and Papa are here.'

'But Papa just stays in his study, working on Louis' scrapbook, and Mama works on her embroidery, and I feel so alone. I don't know how only children bear it.'

Thea smiled. 'Put on your hat and coat. You can't come to the life class, but why don't you go to the library and then we can walk over to Hindley Street together and have a hot drink at West's Coffee Palace.'

Thea had joined the Royal South Australian Society of Arts back in 1915 but now it was the focus of her life outside Larksrest. As the tram rattled into town, Tiney took the Society's newsletter and a catalogue of recent work out of Thea's bag and flipped through the pages. The symbol of the Society was a seated Grecian woman, bare breasted, holding an easel and a palm branch. Even though Tiney knew that Thea never modelled in the life classes, only drew, she couldn't help but think of the goddess as being connected somehow to Thea.

Tiney ran her finger down the list of members, searching for Sebastian Farr's name but he wasn't mentioned. Then she saw the announcement. The Society was calling for entries to their annual prize. There were categories for still life and portraits but the biggest prize was for a landscape. Fifty pounds – half a fare to London. Tiney slipped the newsletter into her bag and then opened up the exhibition catalogue.

Nette and Minna always said the Society was full of stuffy old fuddy-duddies, but since meeting Sebastian at the Alstons' ball, Tiney had begun to think they were quite wrong. There was something romantic about sitting in a room full of people focused on capturing beauty, even if it did mean staring at a nude for hours.

'Is Sebastian Farr a member of the Society?' asked Tiney. 'His name isn't listed in any of these pamphlets.'

Thea blushed and snatched back the exhibition catalogue.

'Candidates have to submit two paintings and have them approved before they can even become an associate member,' she said.

'Will they approve him?'

'Of course he'll be accepted. He was a war artist. His sketches of the battlefields and the men are brilliant.'

Tiney smiled. She'd never seen Thea so animated talking about anyone.

They walked up North Terrace in the crisp evening. Thea hitched her canvas bag of art materials higher over her shoulder. Inside were her sketchbooks, a box of conte and a set of pastels.

The sisters parted ways outside the Society and Tiney wandered over to the library. She climbed the stairs to the third floor. She loved the way the internal balconies wrapped around the walls and the bookshelves rose up to the high ceilings. It began to rain outside. Settled at a desk in a corner between two shelves, Tiney felt unexpectedly happy. The interior of the library was so familiar, like the home of an old friend. When she was small, Louis would bring her here, lift her up high to reach books on shelves out of reach. She would sit quietly reading at a table with him while he studied and afterwards, he would take her down to the coffee palace for a treat. Though the world outside was changing faster than she could bear, inside the library she could feel safe.

Tiney collected several books on nursing. Between the influenza epidemic and the returned wounded soldiers, there was plenty of work in nursing, though the pay was even less than for teachers. After half an hour, she returned the volumes and lapsed into flipping through picture books about France. She drew the Society's newsletter from her bag and smoothed it out on the table in front of her again, studying the information about entering the art prize.

At the appointed time, Tiney skipped down the stairs and

out into North Terrace to find Thea standing with several of the other artists.

She overheard one of the older gentleman say, 'The Society should refuse pictures that are offensive to good taste.'

'Art isn't simply decor,' said Sebastian. 'Surely there's a role for art to provoke.'

'I am a fellow of this Society. If I interpret a work of art as offensive, then I believe it will offend others as well. We shouldn't subject the public to such unpleasantness.'

'Unpleasantness?' said Thea, her voice trembling with barely suppressed rage. 'Mr Farr's work isn't about what's "pleasant". It's about what's true. I'm sure there was nothing pleasant about the trenches. Mud, pain, suffering, death – that was the truth he saw in France and if he chooses to submit his work to the Society we should be honoured to hang it in the Spring Exhibition.'

'Miss Flynn!' said the older gentleman. 'I didn't mean to cast aspersions on Mr Farr's heroism.'

Thea looked flustered and was about to speak again when Ida Alston came flying down the steps of the Society of Arts, almost colliding with the group. She wrapped an arm around Thea and literally dragged her away.

'Sorry to keep you waiting,' she called over her shoulder to Sebastian and Tiney. 'You must all be starving for supper.'

Tiney was relieved by Ida's unexpected rescue. She'd never seen Thea so worked up before. The elderly painter bade them goodbye and Sebastian and Tiney fell into step behind Ida and Thea as they headed along the wet pavement towards West's Coffee Palace on Hindley Street. Tiney looked up at the turrets and flags fluttering in the wintry evening breeze. She glanced ahead at Thea, her face so steely as she brooded on the argument, and then at Sebastian. He was smiling, not at Tiney, but at Thea, as if he were laughing at her.

'Mr Farr, you have to appreciate that my sister is a very serious creature,' said Tiney, almost apologetically.

'Don't call me Mr Farr. I'm only Seb. And there's nothing creature-like about Thea, unless she's a creature such as a butterfly.'

'Thea? A butterfly? Our brother Louis said she was a swan maiden.'

Seb smiled. 'I can see that too. Definitely something beautiful, with wings. Old Oswin managed to ruffle her feathers.'

'That was your fault,' said Tiney. 'She was trying to defend you.'

'There's not a lot of point. The old men always win,' said Seb, his brow suddenly creased. He thrust his hands into his pockets. His pace slowed and he fell behind the girls. As they were about to cross the road, she looked back and saw him standing with his fists clenched, kicking a lamppost with terrible force.

'Seb!' called Thea.

At the sound of her voice, Seb strode to join them but his expression was bleak and he responded brusquely to Thea's gentle questions. Tiney was shocked to see his mood turn so quickly. They walked in silence the rest of the way along Hindley Street.

Inside West's Coffee Palace, trade was slow. Most of the waitresses had been replaced by waiters over the past few months as women gave up their jobs for returned servicemen. The lone waitress, dressed very plainly in a long brown skirt, also wore a face-mask. It was hard to understand her through the gauze covering.

'I suppose we should all drag our face-masks out too,' sighed

Ida. 'It would be just my luck to catch this wretched disease as it starts to wane.'

'We should still be careful,' said Thea. 'Millions have died, mostly people our age.' She reached into her bag and drew out two neatly folded cotton masks.

Tiney screwed up her nose.

'Please, Thea,' she said. 'I can't drink my tea wearing that mask.' Even though Mama had embroidered small flowers on them to make them less drab, Tiney loathed the feel of the cloth against her nose and mouth.

'I think what we all need is a jaunt out of town,' announced Ida. 'Especially you two Flynns. Let's all go down to Christie's Beach. You know Mother and I have a sweet little shack down there, on the clifftops. We could go painting seascapes together. Seb could come too, couldn't you, old digger? If there are three girls to chaperone you, everyone will think you're either an utter roué or an absolute lamb.'

Seb laughed, the moody darkness in his eyes evaporating. *'Three women for every man...'* he sang.

'That's a terrible old song,' admonished Thea.

'I know,' said Seb. 'But I always thought that line about how *"women are angels without wings"* was rather fine.'

Thea laughed and Tiney saw something in her sister that she'd never seen before; something bright and fierce and breathlessly happy.

Rain off the sea beat against the windows of the house at Christie's Beach. It was much nicer than Ida had led them to imagine: a cottage, not a beach shack, with paned windows and whitewashed walls and geraniums scrambling up the back trellis.

Tiney put another log on the fire and looked across the room to where Thea and Seb sat side by side on the sofa. She was glad she'd insisted on being their chaperone. When Ida's mother fell ill and Ida couldn't come on the planned escape, there'd been fleeting talk of finding an elderly relative to accompany the Flynns, but Tiney had talked her parents around. Thea and Seb wouldn't have been able to relax with some old biddy fretting over their every move.

The holiday had been perfect. During the day, they all walked down to the beach and Thea and Seb would set up their camp-stools and easels in the shadow of the chalky, white cliffs. Tiney paddled in the water or read in the shade of a beach umbrella while the two painters worked on their canvases. Sometimes they pencilled her into their sketches. These were the ones that Tiney loved the most.

Thea painted carefully, studying the waves as if they were her infant children. Each brushstroke was placed with a sharp, focused precision. In the same time that it took her to paint a single small canvas, Seb had completed three. Even when the sea was calm, his paintings were infused with restless energy. Though the surface of the water appeared serene, Tiney had the sense that for Seb nothing stayed still. Everything was moving and surging beneath the surface of the calmest seas. His skies were full of bold clouds, the wind tore along the beach, and every detail was infused with movement. The whole canvas seemed to heave with a forceful undercurrent.

When he was done, he would lie beside Thea and watch her work. Sometimes, he leaned forward to study her technique with intense interest and then, if she gazed too long at her subject, he would languidly stretch out at her feet like a gold lion and fall asleep in the white sand.

The third night they were at the cottage, Tiney was wrenched awake by the sound of screaming. It made her heart pound. She glanced across at Thea's bed. Her sister was sitting up, scrabbling for her glasses.

'What was that?'

'Seb,' said Thea. 'It's Seb.' She snatched her kimono dressing gown from the end of the bed and tied the cord quickly.

The girls ran along the narrow hall in the dark, following the painful cries to their source. The screaming made the glass in the windows rattle.

Thea stopped outside Seb's bedroom door. She looked at Tiney, as if she wasn't sure what to do next, then rattled the doorknob.

'It's locked,' she said.

Tiney pushed in front of her and pounded on the timber. 'Seb, Seb, Sebastian,' she called. 'Let us in!'

'It sounds as though someone's torturing him,' said Thea. 'We must wake him.'

'If I go around the side, I might be able to climb in through his window,' said Tiney.

Thea looked appalled. 'You can't do that.' Then Seb let out a heart-stopping cry and Thea gripped Tiney's arm. 'Quickly, I'll give you a leg-up,' she said, dragging Tiney through the front door.

The window was narrow with four small panes and a brass

latch that was loosely fixed to the frame. Tiney and Thea curled their fingers around the edge of the window and wrenched it open. Then Thea boosted Tiney up and over the ledge.

Standing in the small, dark bedroom, Tiney realised that perhaps she should be afraid. She could see the outline of Seb's body thrashing on the narrow metal bunk. She wanted to shake him awake but his flailing limbs alarmed her. She grabbed a jug of water from the dresser, stepped closer to the bed and called his name, staying out of arm's reach. When the screams continued, she tossed the water onto Seb's face. He gasped and shouted as he struggled to consciousness. Tiney leapt away from him, clutching the jug to her chest. Thea, like a ghost at the window, called out, 'Sebastian, it's all right. It's only me and Tiney. We've come to wake you. Quickly, Tiney, open the door for me.'

Then Thea was in the room, sitting on the edge of Seb's bed with her arms around him, as he shivered to waking.

'I'll put the kettle on,' said Tiney, for want of anything better to say or do. In the kitchen, she filled the kettle and set it on the gas. Sitting on a cane chair by the burnt-out fire, her knees pulled up to her chest and her nightgown pulled down over them, Tiney wished she were at home. She shut her eyes and listened to the sound of the sea breaking on Christie's Beach.

When the kettle boiled, she made tea and took it into the bedroom; but she found Seb and Thea asleep on Seb's narrow single bed. Thea lay outside the covers, her arms around Seb, one hand cradling his head. Seb nestled his cheek against her fair hair, his face serenely peaceful as he slept.

Tiney fetched a crocheted blanket from her room and laid it gently over Thea before going back to her own bed.

In the morning, Tiney poured the cold tea-leaves into the bin and sat alone in the small kitchen, watching rain beat against the windowpane. Much later, Seb and Thea finally emerged, looking sheepish and strangely relaxed. There was an ease in Thea that Tiney had never seen, as if her limbs had become more lithe, as if all the tight, intense unhappiness that bound her to her canvases had been swept away.

When the rain had lifted, they all went for a walk along the beach. Tiney ran ahead while Seb and Thea walked behind, holding hands. Tiney felt suddenly lonely in the lovers' company. She left them standing at the water's edge and climbed the path to the clifftop.

On the bus heading back to Adelaide, the sisters sat together. Tiney could feel a crackle of electricity that emanated from the seat in front of them where Seb was sitting alone, reading a book. It was as if his body was sending out invisible waves of heat and energy that made Thea smile and blush.

'Seb,' said Tiney, tapping him on the shoulder. 'Shall we swap seats?'

Seb and Thea slept for the rest of the bus trip, Thea's head settled gently on Seb's shoulder. Tiney knelt on her seat and turned around to watch their faces. They were so beautiful she wished she knew how to draw so she could capture the moment. If Seb and Thea were to marry, it would be the most romantic ceremony. Not like Ray and Nette's wedding, where shadows of doubt had shown on everyone's faces. It would be a union of true souls.

Papa liked Seb from the moment he walked into the house.

Although Seb would deflect any question that Tiney or Thea asked him about his time on the Western Front, on his first visit to Larksrest he spent over an hour in Papa's study talking about the war. Mama loved Seb's gentle good manners.

On Violet Day, a week after they'd returned from Christie's Beach, Seb dropped by Larksrest uninvited, a small bouquet of the purple flowers in his hand. Thea wasn't at home but he spoke with Papa and then took tea with Tiney and Mama in the kitchen, insisting there was no need for them to entertain him in the front parlour. It was as if he were a member of the family already. When Mama asked him how his painting was progressing, he laughed.

'Thea says I must enter work in the Spring exhibition, but I don't think old Oswin will back my inclusion. He seems to find my work too "disturbing".'

'You should submit one of your seascapes,' said Tiney. 'They're beautiful.'

'Thea's are finer. I've never seen anyone capture light on water the way she can.'

'She's finished that canvas she started at Christie's Beach,' said Tiney. 'Come and see. It's on the easel in her studio.'

'Tiney, perhaps you should allow your sister to show Sebastian her own work,' said Mama.

'Thea won't mind,' said Tiney, though a flicker of doubt almost made her sit down again.

Seb followed her across the back garden to Thea's studio. Tiney found the studio key underneath an upturned terracotta pot and unlocked the door. Seb grew quiet, almost reverent, inside the small space. He stood for a long time in front of Thea's canvas, simply staring at the work.

'I wish she'd submit it for the art prize, but she says she doesn't think it's good enough,' said Tiney.

'It's perfection,' said Seb.

'I'd submit pictures on her behalf, but I can't afford the entry fees,' said Tiney.

'I can afford it,' said Seb.

Tiney smiled. 'Can you really? When she wins, we'll pay you back. But Thea mustn't know. And we can't possibly submit this one, she'd notice it was missing. But she has lots of canvases stored in the rack over there.' She began to pull out some of her favourites of Thea's paintings, showing them to Seb with sisterly pride.

'We should put her up for every prize in the country,' said Seb, conspiratorially. 'The Sydney prize has a category for drawings. Thea would be a strong contender. Would she notice if some of her line drawings went missing?'

Tiney clapped her hands. 'Perfect!'

Together, Tiney and Seb sifted through Thea's folios, picking out several works that Seb promised to frame. Tiney took the collection of drawings and two paintings from Thea's store of older works and slipped down the side path with them so Mama wouldn't see Seb carry them through the house. As she snuck beneath the windows, she was reminded of playing hide-and-seek with Louis. It was almost too good to be true that Seb had the same sense of mischief and adventure as her brother.

Tiney spent the rest of the afternoon whistling while she worked at scrubbing the kitchen floor. At dinner, though, she found that Papa was grim with anxiety at the latest news from Germany.

'How can the Germans sign the treaty when Scheidemann and his cabinet have resigned in protest against it?' he said, gloomily.

'The coaltion will have to form a new German government and who knows where that will lead us.'

'But there won't be another war,' said Tiney. 'There can't be.'

'In Paris, General Foch has ordered the mobilisation of the allied armies, and today the Germans scuttled their own ships in Scapa Flow. The German sailors are now prisoners of war. Madness, chaos.'

Tiney wanted to cover her ears. Instead she began clearing the table. As long as she was working, she could keep the dark thought of another war at bay.

Tiney had just drifted off to sleep when the loud trill of the phone echoed through the house. For a moment, she imagined someone was calling to announce the outbreak of war. Thea was first out of bed to answer it. Tiney heard the gentle murmur of her voice and then a horrible sound, like an injured animal wailing in the night. Tiney ran to the door. In the dimly lit hall, Thea lay on the floor in her nightgown, curled into a ball, rocking and moaning. The telephone receiver dangled at the end of its cord and banged against the wall.

Tiney knelt down beside Thea and tried to pull her hands away from her face, to make her speak. Mama and Papa came out of their room, their eyes wide. Mama knelt down on Thea's other side and tried to put her arms around Thea but she wouldn't be comforted. Papa reached for the phone and asked the operator to reconnect him to the previous caller. He listened carefully to the speaker on the other end, then he replaced the receiver.

Mama had gently led Thea into the kitchen and was making

her a cup of warm milk, hoping to coax some sense from her. Papa looked down at Tiney with a numb expression.

'It's Sebastian Farr. He's gone missing. The police believe he has drowned. There was a note, for Thea, among his things.'

Not even the news of peace could lift the darkness that had settled on Larksrest. On the 28th of June, 1919, the Germans signed the Treaty of Versailles but while Thea grieved for Seb, celebrating seemed unkind. Seb's death was almost more than the family could bear.

The police had found Sebastian's clothes, neatly folded in a small pile beside his leather shoes, at the base of the cliffs at Christie's Beach. Ida drove Thea and Tiney down to the cottage at the beginning of July in the hope it would give Thea a chance to grieve properly. Though Adelaide bustled with plans for Peace Day celebrations in late July, Ida decided she would stay with the Flynn sisters at Christie's Beach as long as they needed her.

Thea spent most days standing on the clifftop above Christie's Beach staring out at the horizon. It was frightening for Tiney to see her sister standing so still, so frail, as if an updraft might sweep her into the sky. She wanted to drag Thea inside, to keep her somewhere safe and sheltered.

Every morning, Thea rose at dawn and walked down the winding track to the cliff edge to watch the sea, as if staring might bring Seb back to her, as if the waves might part and she would see him rise from the ocean like a Greek god. And every morning Tiney would follow her, picking her way carefully over rocks and low scrub to watch over her sister and stand vigil.

14

In the olive grove

Tiney heard the front door slam. She stumbled out of bed and pressed her face against the bay window in time to see a figure disappearing down the front path in the moonlight. She thought it would be Thea. Thea who couldn't sleep, who could be found at all hours of the night sitting in her studio, sketching as though only by touching pencil to paper could she keep her grief at bay. But the figure disappearing down the front path wasn't Thea.

'Pa,' whispered Tiney.

Everyone had been so busy worrying about Seb's death and Minna's disappearance that no one but Tiney had noticed the fading of their father. If Tiney asked him to come out for an evening walk, he shook his head and stayed at his desk, sipping at a teacup that Tiney knew held only whisky, not black tea. He sat in his study in a fug of old tobacco and alcohol, making notes in the scrapbook of Louis' life. Not even Mama challenged him, Mama who loved him best.

Tiney had seen he wasn't right. One afternoon, she had found him standing outside Larksrest, staring at the house as if he wasn't sure he lived there. Then he sat down in the gutter like a tramp, like a swagman. Mama had gone outside and spoken to him softly, cajoled him from the gutter and to his desk again. Back in his study, he wrote more letters. Anxious, plaintive letters, asking for more information about Louis' death, but no single detail was enough to sate his longing.

Papa hadn't spoken to anyone for days after he discovered he couldn't collect Louis's effects from the AIF because Louis had written in the Pay Book that his mother was his legatee. Though they'd opened the parcel together, though it was only a formality that the package was addressed to Mama, he questioned why Louis hadn't nominated his father. He combed over each and every memory of Louis' life as though to view it through different prisms.

Every day, he worked on his scrapbooks, adding furious notations. He wouldn't brook conversation about the photo of the woman and child. It puzzled him. It didn't fit among the pieces he was using to shape the history of his son. The records from the Red Cross arrived and a letter from a soldier who had been at Louis' burial. Mama said it was a comfort but Papa said it was a version of a story that thousands had already heard about their sons: the padre said prayers, his mates laid him to rest. They made a cross of wood and painted it. They set it above his grave. As the last of the letters about Louis's death arrived, Pa copied out passages of them into notebooks. He sorted newspaper clippings, sifted through every letter Louis had ever written and wrote up an itinerary of Louis's movements in Belgium and France.

'He was injured here,' said Pa, touching his head, 'and here,' his hand resting on his thigh. 'Some say he died that day, others that it was the day after. Did he speak? Do you think he was in pain?' On and on he went, tormenting himself with the details.

But the detail that frustrated Papa the most was the uncertainty about where Louis was buried. The place was named the 'Buire British Cemetery' but there were so many Buires on the map of northern France that Papa couldn't decide which was the right one. Another report arrived saying the cemetery was near Tincourt, and the whole family puzzled over the map together. Where was Louis? No one could be sure. Once the last letters arrived, something went out of Pa.

Visits from either of the McCaffreys only made things worse. To see living, breathing men return when his only son would never cross the threshold of Larksrest broke something inside him. When Sebastian died, Papa was bewildered and enraged – not only because Thea had been so hurt, but that anyone could come home from the war and throw away a future for which millions of men had fought and died. Seb's death triggered something deep and disturbing in each of the Flynns. The fractures that had riven the family since the news of Louis' death became chasms.

Tiney dressed quickly in the dark, not wanting to wake Thea. The July night was cold. She slipped on a gabardine overcoat, pulled her hair back into a ponytail and flung a scarf over her head. She drew the front door shut as quietly as she could. In the street, there was no sign of her father. She closed her eyes, trying to intuit which way he might have walked. He always turned left if he was going for a long walk through the parklands to eventually reach the river Torrens. If he was going to North Adelaide, he'd turn to the right. But it was the middle of the night. Why would he be going in either direction? Instinctively, Tiney turned right and hurried towards Robe Terrace. The wide street was empty. In the far distance she could see the lights of a brougham cab. A half-moon cast a thin light across the parklands.

Tiney could make out a dark figure moving slowly across the Pound Paddock, the wide stretch of raggedy grassland that separated Medindie from North Adelaide. The park had grown wilder during the war years, the grass a home for snakes, the paths untended. Tiney and her sisters avoided it. Clutching the collar of her coat she hurried across Robe Terrace, following her father.

At first she thought he was heading towards North Adelaide, and her heart sank. She couldn't bear the thought of having to retrieve him from inside an illegal speakeasy, a dark and gloomy cellar, rank with the stench of alcohol. Frank had told her about those places, where returned soldiers went to drown their misery.

She quickened her pace, hoping to catch him before he crossed LeFevre Terrace, but as the gap closed between them, she became less sure of his direction. He seemed to be wandering in a purposeless fashion, weaving between the trees, disappearing into the shadow of a gum and then reappearing further east towards Kingston Terrace. It was only as he drew nearer to North Adelaide that Tiney realised they were not alone. There were two other figures wandering in among the trees in the darkness of the night. Tiney tried to keep her gaze fixed steadily on her father. She didn't want to think of why there were other men in the park in the middle of the night, nor of what they might do to her if they decided to accost her. She broke into a run, racing to catch up with her father as he crossed into the top end of North Adelaide. He had quickened his pace too and she was just in time to see him turn left into a side street.

It was a relief to be out of the parklands and away from the shadowy wandering men, but now she had lost sight of Papa. She stood clutching a fencepost, catching her breath. She had no idea her father could move so swiftly. She wondered if she could actually catch up with him. But the thought of abandoning the chase and then having to cross the Pound Paddock and return home without her father was more frightening than wandering through the sleeping streets of the town. As she debated what to do, Tiney noticed something odd. Though it was after two a.m., there were men as purposeless as her father wandering the streets. When she turned into Stanley Street and nearly collided with a young man, the man apologised gruffly, shoved his hands deeper into his pockets and kept walking. He neither registered nor cared that Tiney was a young woman alone.

Tiney heard a clock chime the hour. Three o'clock. Was this what the town was always like in the middle of the night, the darkness peppered with men wandering wild-eyed? She saw a man sitting in his dimly lit living room, framed by a window, his head in his hands. She heard a baby cry. A dog bark. Then to her relief she caught sight of Papa again, crossing over into the park, into the olive groves.

Papa had loved to take them for picnics in the olive groves when they were little. Nette and Ma thought it a shoddy place for a picnic. Why not the riverbank? Or the Botanical Gardens? But Pa like the wild scruffiness of the olive grove with its dips and hollows and dry yellow grass. He would tell them that the first Europeans to come to Adelaide had planted the grove and that the trees would still be there in thousands of years, like the Garden of Gethsemane. He told them it was a place where spirits roamed, where a man could find his god.

Tiney knew where her father would be heading for now.

There was a rock that Louis had liked to sit upon whenever they visited the grove as a family. Papa had christened it Louis' Rock.

In a hollow between the twisted olives, Tiney found her father. His black hair had turned silver these past months, his eyes sunken deeper into his face. His hands were knotted together, as if in prayer, though she knew her Pa never prayed. She stood in front of him and slipped the scarf from her head so he could see her face in the moonlight.

'Papa,' she whispered. When he didn't look at her, she put a hand on his shoulder. 'Pa, we should go home. There are men, walking about in the streets. I think they're soldiers. I want you to walk home with me.'

She sat down on the rock beside him and slid her arm around his shoulders. He was trembling and muttering to himself. She leaned her ear close, to hear his voice. *'Father, if thou wilt, remove this chalice from me . . . And there appeared to him an angel from heaven . . . And being in an agony, he prayed the longer. And his sweat became as drops of blood, trickling down upon the ground.'*

Then he turned and looked straight into Tiney's face and said again, *'Drops of blood, trickling down upon the ground.* The Garden of Gethsemane and the Rock of Agony.'

For the first time that evening, Tiney felt truly afraid.

'Don't, Pa,' she said. 'You shouldn't have come out, you're not well.'

'Where can we go to mourn him? There's nowhere to go. No place to remember him. Do you remember him here, in the olive grove?'

The moonlight caught the fever glistening in her father's eyes. He coughed and shivered again.

'We have to get you home,' she said, wedging herself beneath her father's arm and standing up, forcing him to his feet. The top of her head barely reached his shoulder but it meant she was the perfect size to act as a crutch. All her fear was overridden by a sense of urgency.

Normally she would have taken two steps for every one of her father's, but that night his gait was reduced to a shuffle. She tried not to listen to his ravings. He muttered of tombs and blood and sacrifice, and coughed and wept.

Tiney kept her head down. The tie in her hair fell out. She dropped her scarf. But still she kept walking, past the lonely wandering men in Stanley Street, through the Pound Paddock, ignoring the shadows and her fears. By the time she finally led Papa under the portico at Larksrest, she didn't care if she woke the whole house. She lifted the brass knocker and banged it down hard.

When Thea opened the door, Tiney wanted to cry but instead she spoke urgently. 'I think Pa has the influenza,' she said, keeping terror from her voice.

Tiney slept heavily but only for a few hours. She woke at dawn. Thea wasn't in her bed beneath the window. Tiney put on her dressing gown and stepped out into the hall. In the kitchen, her mother was at the stove and the kettle was boiling on the hob, sending up a plume of steam into the crisp morning air.

Across the hallway, their father lay in the cot in his study. Thea sat in a chair beside him, a small bowl of water in her lap. She dipped a cloth into it and wiped Pa's brow. His face was a strange colour, almost blue, and a tiny fleck of foamy blood was caught in his beard. Thea wiped it away as Tiney drew close.

'Mama called the doctor but he can't come until later,' said Thea.

'But we need him now!' said Tiney, alarmed by how much worse Papa had grown in the course of a few hours.

'I wish Nette was here,' said Thea, lowering her voice. 'We need Nette.'

'You know she can't come to Adelaide with the baby while the influenza is still raging,' said Tiney. 'It's Minna we need. She's the one Papa misses most. We need Minna to come home.'

Papa made a desperate gargling sound in the back of his throat and shuddered. Thea looked at Tiney and put her finger to her lips. Papa began to shiver, his whole body trembling and shaking until the bed began to knock against the wall.

'Mama!' called Tiney, as she and Thea tried to loosen their father's shirt. Mama came into the room with a bowl of cold water and cloths.

'We must bring his fever down,' she said.

Together, Thea, Tiney and Mama wiped his trembling limbs with cool water. When Papa seemed less feverish, Mama covered him with a cotton sheet. Mama and Thea carried the cloths and bowls from the room. Tiney pulled a chair away from her father's desk and sat beside his bed to keep vigil.

By the time the doctor arrived, Papa had lapsed into a rattling, restless sleep. The doctor said there was no point in taking Papa to the overcrowded hospital when he had three women to nurse him at home. He placed a quarantine order on Larksrest and instructed each of them to take every precaution to protect themselves from the disease. It killed the young and healthy even more quickly than older adults. They would know in ten days whether Papa would improve or whether his condition would worsen, if and when pneumonia took hold. Tiney went to her room and took the cotton mask that Mama had embroidered with pale blue flowers from the chest of drawers. A choking sob rose up in her chest as she tied it in place.

They divided the days into shifts where each of them took turns to sit beside Papa. They were the longest ten days of Tiney's life. Tiney took the night shifts, determined that Papa wouldn't be left alone for a moment. Her father had done the same for her and the story of her birth was etched so deep in family lore, she knew she owed her life to Papa.

When Tiney was born, the doctor thought there was no hope for her. She had come too early into the world, her eyes shut tight like a baby kitten, her body covered with fine dark hair. The doctor had told her parents to keep her safely at home with them until she died because surely a baby so premature couldn't possibly survive. But Papa was stubborn. He had put Tiney in a shoebox and sat beside the stove for a month. When the nights grew cold, he would place his youngest daughter, wrapped in a soft pink wool rug, on the edge of a spade and hold her over the rising warmth from the woodstove. Slowly, over the weeks she shed her downy black hair. Papa fed her with an eyedropper to begin with and then from a tiny spoon. His patience and pig-headedness gave Tiney her life. The least she could do for him was to match his devotion all these years later.

Slowly, in small steps, Papa began to recover. He stopped his ravings, the fever abated and he lapsed into a state of quiet exhaustion.

The doctor's bills were frightening. Bottles of Nutone Brain and Nerve Tonic cost half a crown for one single pint. It saved on buying lots of little bottles but when Papa finished the first course the doctor suggested another, so yet another half-crown had to be taken out of the household budget.

The Alstons left a care parcel on the front steps, but no one would come to the house to visit while it was officially in quarantine. Only Frank McCaffrey crossed the threshold, against advice. He would come from the Adelaide Markets, with a basket of fresh fruit over one arm and a bag full of bottles of aerated water in the other. Even though he hadn't known Seb or Louis very well, he spoke of them with ease, as if they were old friends. When the screen door broke in a high wind, Frank came with his toolbag and repaired it.

Then, on a bright July morning, when Papa was sitting up in bed and Tiney arranging a vase of jonquils to cheer his room, they heard the doorbell ring and Frank's voice in the hall. Thea called for Tiney to join them in the breakfast room. Tiney kissed Papa on the forehead and promised she would be back in a minute.

Frank was sitting at the end of the table, his hat on a chair while Mama and Thea sat either side of him. For a moment, Tiney's heart leapt. Frank had something to say to her, something terribly important. But surely he should ask her in private? Then she saw the letter: a single page spread out on the table in front of Frank. He laid his palm on the smooth lavender-coloured sheet.

'I've found Minna,' he said.

15

Peace Day, 1919

Tiney watched Frank as he slept, his head propped up on a folded coat. When he had announced that he and Thea were going to Melbourne to find Minna and bring her home, something inside Tiney broke. She felt it snap as she suddenly realised she had misunderstood something very deep about the nature of their friendship. It was an added humiliation that she had to beg to be included in the search party. She stared out into the darkened countryside as the South Australian landscape sped past. The long nights of nursing Papa had made it hard for her to sleep and it was only as dawn light crept across the bush that she finally nodded off.

'We're here,' said Frank, touching Tiney gently on the shoulder to rouse her. Tiney rubbed the back of her neck, stiff from sleeping upright. Her cheek felt cold and numb where it had pressed against the train window. She stared at the grubby railway yards, the miles of tracks and ugly black and brown stones, and the smog of a real city. 'Where should we begin?' she asked.

'First we've got to get you two settled in,' said Frank. He picked up Tiney's small suitcase and Thea's easel. Tiney and Thea followed him along the platform and out into Spencer Street.

They caught a tram up Collins Street, past elegant shops and leafless winter elms. Even though it was still early, the streets were bustling. Buildings were decked with flags and coloured streamers and people were setting up chairs on rooftops and balconies. Red, white and blue bunting was splashed across shopfronts. Banners bearing the names of all the principal battles fought and won by Australian troops were stretched across the streets. Bands warmed up on street corners and people broke into patriotic song. Tiney wondered how they could possibly find Minna in a city so crowded.

Through friends at the Society of Arts, Thea had organised a room for them in a boarding house in East Melbourne.

'You get yourself freshened up,' said Frank, 'and we'll walk back into the city. Almost everything will be shut for the parade but I've arranged to meet a lady at the Theosophical Society. I know Minna's been to at least one of their meetings. They should be able to give us a lead.'

Upstairs in their room, Tiney looked out the window to watch Frank waiting patiently for them in the morning sunshine.

'I still don't understand why Minna wrote to Frank and not to us,' said Tiney. 'If one of the reasons she ran away was to escape George's attention, surely she wouldn't want to write to his brother.'

'Everyone trusts Frank,' said Thea as she filled the china basin on the dresser and began to wash her face.

'She could trust us, too!' said Tiney.

'Could she, Tiney?' said Thea. 'Could she trust you?'

Tiney hung her head. Thea had discovered that Seb had submitted her work for the Society of Arts prize the day he died and that some of her drawings were found among his things. She'd quietly withdrawn the work from the competition. Tiney had apologised, had tried to explain, but a chill had settled over their relationship.

'We should have quizzed Tilda Constance-Higgens right from the start!' said Tiney, hoping to turn the conversation in a different direction.

'We already know she left with Minna. Mama spoke with Mrs Constance-Higgens. She simply didn't tell you.'

Tiney felt stung to the core. 'Why not?'

'Because you might tell someone or take it on yourself to go and find Minna on your own,' said Thea. 'It's not up to you to fix everything in our family.'

Tiney walked disconsolately behind Thea and Frank as they wove their way down Bourke Street, constantly jostled by people gathering for the Peace Day parade. Outside the Theosophical Society headquarters, Frank stopped and turned his gaze skywards. Tiney was struck by how handsome he looked with the sun making his red hair glow.

'There are six planes up there,' said Frank, pointing. 'Looks like they're going to do some nosedives over the city.'

'I'm sorry we're missing the Adelaide parade,' said Tiney.

'For a strike-stricken city, Melbourne's not doing too badly with their Peace Day festivities. We'll make sure you get an eyeful of the fun tonight,' he said, 'whether we find Minna or not.'

'Maybe we'll find her. Maybe we'll be able to really celebrate,' said Tiney as she mounted the stairs to the Theosophical Society.

Inside, they found a small woman in glasses sitting behind a typewriter. Thea and Tiney explained that they were searching for their sister and asked if she had attended any events at the

Theosophical Society. The secretary drew a leather-bound book from a drawer and scanned through lists of names, but Minna wasn't there. Tiney noticed one name that was easy to recognise, even upside down.

'Tilda Constance-Higgens,' said Tiney. 'We know her. She's a friend of ours from Adelaide. Can you tell us how we can get in contact with her?'

'We don't have her current address but I believe she does tarot readings at The Esplanade in St Kilda. She's there on Saturdays.'

Tiney turned to Frank and Thea and smiled.

The tram crossed over the Yarra River and rattled along St Kilda Road, past grand buildings with towers and turrets and an old bluestone barracks where soldiers were gathering for the parade. They climbed down from the tram in Fitzroy Street as a cold gust of air swept up from the bay. Thea stood transfixed by the glittering sea.

Inside the wide foyer of the hotel, potted palms lined the walls and in the far corner, a palm court orchestra was playing.

Frank made enquiries about Tilda but the waiter he spoke with shook his head. Then Tiney interrupted. 'I'd like my fortune told. I believe someone here can help me.'

'Not strictly legal, is it?' said the waiter. But he led them to the back of the foyer. Sitting in a booth, partially shielded by a red curtain, was Tilda Constance-Higgens.

She smiled, not the least surprised by her visitors. 'The cards predicted I'd have interesting clients today.' She gestured for the three of them to sit down.

'Then you know why we're here,' said Frank.

'And you are Frank McCaffrey,' said Tilda.

'No prizes for guessing that if you've been speaking with

Minna. Not many Adelaide diggers with red hair who'd be chaperoning the Flynn girls.'

Tilda smiled, a cat-like smirk that annoyed Tiney.

'I have no idea where Minna is,' said Tilda.

'But you came to Melbourne with her,' said Tiney. 'You must have some idea where we could start looking.'

'I came to Melbourne to help lost souls,' said Tilda. 'I can help you too, Tiney Flynn. Let me cast your tarot.'

'Tilda, I don't want my fortune told. I want to find my sister!' Tiney was conscious of being too loud in her frustration.

The red curtain was drawn back. 'Everything all right here, Miss Constance-Higgens?' asked the waiter.

Tilda nodded and handed Tiney the tarot cards. 'Hold your question in your mind, Tiney, while you shuffle the cards and then cut the pack.'

Tiney glanced up at the waiter and then at Thea and Frank.

'It can't hurt,' said Thea.

Tiney cut the deck and handed it back to Tilda, who drew seven cards from the top of the pack and laid them out in the shape of a horseshoe. She pointed to the first card. 'The Devil reveals an imprudent undertaking. This card is the past, not the future.'

Tilda pointed to the second card. 'The Seven of Swords – lies, rumours, unkind criticism, an unlucky gambler. This is the present moment, a caution about whom you criticise.' She looked sharply at Tiney and Tiney blushed.

'The Magician – he seeks answers and indicates that you may find what you are looking for. This card augurs well for your quest. The fourth card is the Female Pope but she is reversed, which means you mustn't trust your intuition. Three of

Pentacles, reversed, your fifth card, indicates your companions are not reliable.'

At this, Frank snorted with irritation. 'Do we have to go on with this?'

'As I said, your companions are not reliable,' said Tilda. 'They may betray you. But they are not the obstacles. The seventh card shows The Tower — meaning that violent change lies between you and your fate. This is the most dangerous card in the whole tarot. But your last card, Death, this is a good sign.'

'How can that be a good sign?' asked Tiney.

'Because it means rebirth. Not an end but a new beginning, for the person you seek and for you as well.'

Thea leaned forward across the table. 'Tilda, why are you being so obstructive?' She picked up the card with the Female Pope on it and reversed it in front of Tilda. 'Lack of foresight — that's what she means reversed, doesn't she? I think you show a particular lack of foresight if you won't tell us what you know about Minna.'

Tilda swept the cards off the velvet tablecloth and put them into a small drawstring bag. 'I will never betray her.'

Tiney leaned across the table and grasped Tilda's hands. 'We are her family, Tilda,' she said with urgency. 'We love her and we want to help her.'

Tilda smiled into Tiney's eyes for a long moment, as if she found Tiney terribly amusing. Tiney wanted to slap her but instead she let go of Tilda's hands and stood up abruptly.

'Let's go,' said Tiney, pushing aside the velvet curtain.

The palm court orchestra was playing 'Your Eyes are the Light of my World' with a clarinet soloing the melody. 'That was Minna's favourite,' said Frank.

Instantly they all looked towards the stage.

'It's Minna!' said Tiney.

'Wait until she's finished her set,' said Thea, holding Tiney firmly by the arm. They stood watching, their throats dry with anxiety, until the song was at an end. Frank was the first to race across the dance floor, colliding with a waiter and sending a tray of teacups flying. There was a hurried exchange of angry words. By the time all three of them had reached the stage, Minna had disappeared.

'She must have seen you,' said Tiney. 'But why would she run away from you? It's George she's scared of. Is there something you haven't told us?'

Frank sat down on a chair and put his head in his hands.

'We're engaged,' said Frank, in a flat monotone. 'But when George found out, he threatened to kill me. Kill us both. So Minna bolted.'

Thea and Tiney looked at each other, astonished.

'That's why she wrote to me. To let me know she was safe.'

'But she didn't write to us!' said Tiney, suddenly angry. And there was something else, some other emotion so painful stirring in her that she couldn't give voice to it.

'I wanted to tell her to contact you, but she didn't send a return address. I wanted to tell her that I've sorted things with George. He's not right, George. He'll never be right but I found him work up north and he won't bother us. If Minna would only let me explain, everything would be fine.'

Tiney wanted to shout at him, 'Nothing will ever be fine ever again!' But she turned away and stared blankly at the waiter gathering up the shards of broken teacups.

Thea went straight to the bandleader and started asking questions in her quiet, direct manner. Five minutes later, she came back to tell them that Minna was now Minnie La Rue. The bandmaster didn't know where she lived, but he said she also played with the Tivoli Orchestra. 'She'll be there tonight,' said Thea. 'He says they're doing a special show for the Peace Day celebrations.'

They walked down Fitzroy Street to the sea front and Frank bought a parcel of fish and chips for them to share, but Tiney had lost her appetite. She wanted to love being there with Frank, sitting beside him, looking out over the bay, but everything had changed.

It was growing dark by the time they caught the tram back to the city but several blocks short of Flinders Street Station the tram came to a stop and the conductor leaned out the open door to see what was going on.

'Crikey!' he shouted. 'There's a great mob out there and they've derailed the tram up ahead.'

Frank, Thea and Tiney and all the other passengers disembarked. The air was full of the shouts of men. Outside the Victoria Barracks, returned sailors and servicemen were shouting and jostling each other, surging towards the bluestone entrance. Police officers with batons marched towards the angry mob. Frank put an arm around each of the girls, trying to shelter them as they struggled through the crowd. Within minutes of making their way onto Princes Bridge, they heard gunshots, screaming and the noise of battle.

'We better get off the streets,' said Frank. 'If we can make it to the Tivoli and buy tickets, we'll be right.'

But as they walked up Swanston Street, they realised nothing in Melbourne was right. The Peace Day bunting and decorations had been torn down. Plate-glass shop windows were smashed. The band on the balcony of the Town Hall played on, but could hardly be heard; fights were breaking out between men with bottles and police wielding batons, and the screams of women and children filled the air.

Frank herded Tiney and Thea into a doorway as a volley of projectiles – bottles, rocks and even a wheel torn from a baby carriage – flew in their direction.

'What's happened?' asked Tiney.

'The diggers are angry, disappointed,' said Frank.

'But there was just a grand parade in their honour!' said Tiney.

'Parades aren't worth much if you can't find work or a place to live,' said Frank. 'The men are bitter about what's happened since they came home.'

'But this is madness, Frank!' said Tiney.

'I'm not arguing with you.'

They turned the corner into Collins Street to reach the Tivoli Theatre. Tiney saw a young man, not much older than she was, raising a bottle to throw at a police officer.

'Stop!' she cried. The young man looked surprised, and lowered his arm to stare at her. 'This isn't the way,' she said, breaking away from Frank and Thea. 'This isn't going to help find you work or help us rebuild the country!'

The man seemed momentarily contrite but then an older woman came out of the darkness and shouted, 'Don't listen to the likes of them, lad. You fight for your rights.'

The young man dashed after the policeman and set upon him with his fists. Frank grabbed Tiney's hand and dragged her up the steps of the Tivoli. For a split second Tiney thought they had found safety. Instead, they found the ticket-seller weeping inside her booth. There were no ushers and the foyer had an air of disarray. From inside the theatre they could hear shouts and jeering.

'We want tickets,' said Thea. 'For the show.'

'You'd be the first to pay for them,' said the young woman. 'The diggers stormed the theatre. The ushers couldn't stop them. They've taken over the place and we're all scared out of our wits. I don't know where to hide. I'm too scared to go home through that mob outside.'

'But our sister is inside! She's playing with the orchestra. We have to get her out of there,' said Tiney.

'I can't help you,' said the woman. She pulled down the shutter and disappeared from view.

'I should take you two back to East Melbourne right now,' said Frank. 'The city's gone mad.'

'We can't give up,' said Tiney. 'Minna is in there somewhere. We can't just leave her to the mob. Why don't you go home to bed. We'll find her without you.'

'Stop it, Tiney,' said Thea. 'We couldn't do this without Frank.'

They made their way into the theatre and stood in the aisle, on the far side of the stalls, watching as a performer came out on stage and pleaded with the angry audience to calm down. He could hardly be heard above the roar and stamping of feet, the diggers demanding the show begin. Finally, the actor managed to make himself heard above the catcalls and boos. He announced the performers had been promised a share of the takings and asking them to perform for free was unjust; if the diggers had paid for their tickets it would be a different story. The soldiers seemed momentarily shamed. Up in the balcony, a slouch hat was hurriedly passed around.

Tiney looked up and saw the slouch hat kicked into the air on the boot of a soldier. Coins and pound notes flew out over the stalls and landed in the audience. Immediately there was a scrum of men falling upon each other, scrabbling for the cash. The actor on stage threw his hands up in despair and signalled to the conductor for the orchestra to strike up a tune.

That's when Tiney saw Minna, dressed in black, sitting in the orchestra pit. Before either Thea or Frank could stop her, Tiney dashed down the aisle and tried to lunge over the side of the barrier.

'Minna!' screamed Tiney, as a burly digger grabbed her arm, holding her back.

Minna glanced up, shocked. Then she jumped to her feet, pushed past the other musicians, leaned over the barrier and raised her clarinet like a bludgeon above the head of the man restraining Tiney. 'Let go of my baby sister, you brute!' she said.

The man glanced at Minna's angry face and released Tiney. She flung her arms around Minna's neck.

'Minna,' she said, kissing her sister's cheek. 'Come home to us. Come home right now, please.'

'I can't, darling. Not until after the show.'

'No, now, Minna,' said Tiney, holding fast. 'You have to come now!'

Minna glanced back at the conductor.

'Sorry, Mac!' she shouted. Then she hoisted herself up onto the barrier and jumped over.

'Let's get out of this madhouse,' said Minna.

As they raced up the aisle, Frank ran towards them and swept Minna into his arms. To the hoots and catcalls of the soldiers, he kissed her full on the mouth. Minna clung to him and kissed him right back. Tiney didn't know where to look.

Twenty minutes later, they were settled at a table in a small back-street club off Little Bourke Street. Frank bought a lemon squash for Tiney, a shandy for Thea and Minna and a beer for himself. Tiney looked around the smoky club in surprise. 'Isn't it against the law to sell beer after six o'clock?'

'I don't think anyone in this town is worrying about the law tonight,' said Frank.

Tiney reached for Minna's shandy and swallowed a mouthful, eyeing her sisters defiantly. It was sweet and bitter in the same instance.

Sunshine in the Riverina

Tiney wiped dust away from her face with the back of her hand. She was glad the noise of the truck engine made it impossible to have a conversation with Ray. She couldn't think how to explain why she was coming alone to Cobdolga without any of her sisters.

It was as if her family had been swept away by the winds of change in one cataclysmic month. Frank and Minna had come home to Adelaide for only two weeks before their hurried marriage in a registry office and then departure for Melbourne, where Frank had found a new job. Worse still, Thea went with them. Thea had met a small group of artists who painted Melbourne rivers and beaches and she had arranged to work with them. As she packed up her studio, Tiney sat on a stool and tried to persuade her to stay but Thea quietly resisted her arguments. Tiney felt Thea had never fully forgiven her for conspiring with Seb to enter her work in competitions, nor had she recovered from his death.

Tiney was the last one left at Larksrest. For more than a month she moped around the house until Mama insisted that now was the time for her to visit Nette. Papa was still too weak to travel and someone had to stay to care for him, so it was up to Tiney to visit her eldest sister and tell her in person about the events of the past two months. Mama also gave firm instructions that Tiney was to bring back an honest description of the house that Ray had built for his wife and baby. Nette's letters were worryingly short on the details of their situation.

Ray's truck screeched to a halt and Tiney took a good look at the 'new house'. It had four walls and a roof, all of corrugated iron, but beyond that, it fell far short of her expectations. It sat in the middle of a wide, red field beneath a searingly sunlit sky.

Ray had planted groves of citrus as far as the eye could see but the irrigation that the government had promised still hadn't been developed. To keep the young trees alive, Ray carted water from the river and hand-watered every day. Beside the house he'd also planted a clutch of gum trees to provide future shade, but in the heat of the day they looked thin and forlorn. Tiney's image of a grove of orange trees smelling sweetly of blossom evaporated instantly, replaced by the stark, sunburnt reality.

Despite the huge swell of her pregnant belly, Nette looked thinner. Her cheekbones stood out far more than they used to, and her hands were red and sinewy. But she folded Tiney in an embrace that was warm and welcoming, and when Tiney pressed her face against her sister's neck it was as if all the pain and worry of the last year floated up into the bright Riverina sky.

Inside the house, Ray had erected a flimsy wall between the main living area and the bedroom. Tiney thought it far from a proper house for a family. The walls weren't lined yet, and a single gold-framed painting by Thea, of the jacaranda tree in bloom at Larksrest, made the absence of plaster and paint even more glaring. But the room was tidy, with shelves displaying canisters of flour, sugar and tea and neatly stacked tinned food.

Sparkling clean crockery lined the dresser in defiance of the dust and there was a carefully arranged single shelf of books. Tiney noticed the smoothly pressed tablecloth that had come from Larksrest. 'You've made it all look so lovely, Nette,' she said, trying to sound convincing.

'When Ray builds another room for us, we'll be able to take down the partition wall and bring the piano up from Larksrest,' said Nette.

Tiney peered around the partition wall. There was a new wicker bassinet sitting beside the couple's sagging double bed, waiting for the baby's arrival.

'I'll make you up a camp bed for tonight and tomorrow. I'm sorry you can't stay longer, Tiney. I wish you could. I've been longing for visitors but Ray says we don't have enough room.'

'We've been longing for you to come home to visit *us*,' said Tiney. 'Mama is so worried about you.'

'I couldn't travel while the flu epidemic was raging and then, just when I thought it was easing and it would be safe to come home, Papa fell ill.'

Tiney took her sister's hand and stroked it. 'It's just I miss you so much.'

'I will come home *after* I've had the baby,' said Nette. 'I'll be constantly in your way, and the babe and I will drive you bonkers.'

'Never,' said Tiney, laughing. They sat at the table in the hot little hut and drank black tea and talked and talked and Tiney told Nette everything. She spoke of the tragedy of Seb and Thea, of Papa's illness, of the hunt for Minna and how empty Larksrest had become, now that she was the last in their family nest, alone with their parents in the old home that had once held five children.

'It's all happening so fast,' said Tiney. 'It was as if the war held us in a cocoon but since it's ended, everyone has taken flight, except me. The flight of the swan maidens.'

They both laughed then. 'And now I'm about to have my own little cygnet,' said Nette. 'I hope it's a girl.'

'Why?'

'Ray says we should call the baby Louis if it's a boy, but I don't think I want that. I'd rather call him Floyd – something modern. I don't want to think of Louis every time I put my baby to my breast. I don't want to imagine a future where a war might snatch him from us. They've made such a hash of the treaty. What if there's another war? I couldn't bear it, Tiney.'

Tiney stared out through the flywire screen at the hot, dusty landscape. 'What would you call her if she was a girl?'

'I'd call her Joy. Because if this baby doesn't bring us joy, I don't know how we'll manage.' Nette put her head down on the tablecloth and began to weep, suddenly changing from laughter to tears.

Tiney stood up and rubbed her sister's shoulders. 'Don't cry, Nette. Joy is a lovely name. And I'm sure if you want to call a baby boy something other than Louis, Ray won't mind. '

'But you don't understand. Ray minds everything. Everything exasperates him. I can't argue with him, I can't. He's angry all the time. It's the land and the heat and that we never have enough water. Oh Tiney, how am I going to manage a baby in this terrible place?'

Tiney stood, stunned, her hands resting on her sister's shoulders. She went on rubbing Nette's back soothingly, but she couldn't help thinking Nette was right. The hut was more like a prison camp than a home, only made liveable through Nette's work and care.

'Why don't you come home to Larksrest to have the baby? You could come back with me. We could be home by Friday,' said Tiney.

Nette continued to weep. 'Because Ray wouldn't like it. It would make him feel angrier. Don't think I haven't already asked. But he wouldn't even talk about it. I've never seen anyone so angry before. He goes out into the fields and it's as if he's marching against some invisible enemy. Sometimes I think it's me, that I'm the new enemy. But then he can be so sweet. I never know which way he's going to be when he comes in at night. And if he's angry, then he drinks. Not like Pa. Pa was always so quiet if he had a drink, but with Ray it's like throwing petrol on a fire. I have to go to bed and pretend I'm alone, pretend I can't hear him shouting and cursing on the other side of the curtain.'

Part of Tiney wanted to say, 'Don't tell me this.' But instead, she said, 'You must come home, Nette. Not just when you're having the baby, but for good. Ray will be a terrible father. You can't live like this. You can't make your baby suffer as well as you.'

There was a silence before Nette spoke. 'You don't leave your wounded,' she said, so still, so quietly, that Tiney wasn't sure she'd heard right. Then Nette looked into Tiney's eyes, holding her gaze, and spoke firmly. 'You don't leave your wounded behind.'

'The war is over, Nette!'

'It will never be over for Ray,' said Nette. She put both hands squarely on the table, as if to signal the end of the conversation. Then she pushed herself to her feet. It was as she stood that they both heard an audible 'pop'. Nette's eyes grew wide and she stared down at her skirt. Tiney followed her gaze. Gathering between Nette's feet was a pool of water, staining the floorboards dark brown.

'My waters have broken,' said Nette disbelievingly.

'What?' said Tiney.

'The baby is coming,' said Nette, cupping her hands under the swell of her belly. 'Fetch Ray, Tiney. Fetch him now.'

Tiney stared at her sister and then out the small window at the bright, hot day. 'But where is he?'

'Down by the river. He'll be down by the river, carting water for the orchard.' Then Nette groaned and leaned forward, both hands on the table, as a contraction gripped her. Tiney watched the force of the moment wash over her, too frightened to leave.

'Go!' shouted Nette, as soon as she could catch her breath.

Tiney stepped out into the bright noonday sun. She ran through the infant orange grove where the ground was cracked and dry, leaping over furrows of baked earth, brushing past the shrivelled citrus trees that were struggling to take hold in the parched ground. She raced towards the line of gums that was the river's edge, screaming Ray's name as she ran.

It took over an hour of frantic searching along the riverbank, scrambling over the roots of river gums, for Tiney to find Ray. When the truck stalled on the road back through the fields, she wanted to scream with both fear and frustration.

By the time they returned to the hut, Nette was bellowing. A carpetbag sat open on the table. She had stopped halfway through packing. She stood with her hands on the back of a chair, her face flushed and sweaty, her cropped hair plastered to her forehead. 'Too fast,' she muttered. 'It's coming too fast.'

'Help me get her to the truck,' said Ray, grabbing one of Nette's arms.

Nette groaned. 'Too late,' she said between gritted teeth. But Ray was hauling her towards the open door.

'Ray, stop,' said Tiney. 'She doesn't want to go.'

'She can't have it here. We've got to get her to the hospital.'

Tiney rested her hand on her sister's rock-hard belly. Nette had taken off her shoes and stockings, and her bare legs were streaked with blood. Tiney took a deep breath and raised her sister's skirts, squatting down to look upward.

'I can see the baby's head. I can see the crown of its head,' she said, feeling her heart swell with despair at the sight of her sister's bulging vulva and the thick thatch of black hair.

'Jesus,' said Ray.

Tiney felt her own smallness, their shared inadequacy.

'You're a farmer, Ray,' said Tiney. 'You should know about how animals are born.'

'I know about bloody oranges,' he shouted, 'not babies! You're a woman. This is woman's business.'

Tiney wanted to shout back, 'I'm only seventeen!' But she realised she knew more than Ray. She'd read a little about babies being born, couched in flowery terms. She knew that she needed to boil water and that things needed to be clean and sterile.

Between them, Ray and Tiney manoeuvred Nette towards the bed, but then she knelt on the floor beside it. She roared in pain and tore at the quilted bedcover. Then she grabbed Ray's hand and Tiney's forearm, dragging them down to kneel beside her. When the contraction had eased and Nette's grip loosened, Tiney raced to the stove and tipped a jug of water into the kettle to boil.

Ray looked at Tiney. She'd never seen his expression so help-less.

'We'll all be fine,' said Tiney, rolling up her sleeves as if she was confident, as if she knew what to do, scrubbing her hands at the sink. Inside her head a voice screamed, 'You have no idea what you're doing!' as she folded back her sister's skirts again and knelt behind her. Nette roared, a shout so loud that the tiny house trembled and all the colour drained from Ray's face. Tiney watched as a damp, glistening head emerged from between her sister's legs. She touched it gently, reverently. In the next moment, Nette roared again and the baby's body slithered from inside her and into Tiney's hands. It was warm and soft and magically alive.

Tiney turned the baby over and saw he was a boy; a perfectly formed baby with long fingers and a squashed, snub nose. She looked down into his face, greasy with a white slick, and the baby opened his eyelids to gaze up at her with cloudy blue eyes. Then he opened his mouth and a mewling cry came from between his lips. Tiney began to weep, tears streaming down her cheeks. She looked across at Ray and he too was weeping. She handed the baby to him, saw how small he looked in his father's hands.

'It's a little boy,' she said, rubbing her sister's back soothingly. 'It's a beautiful little boy, Nette.'

Nette's legs trembled and she buried her face in the quilt. Ray handed back the baby to Tiney and managed to carefully lift Nette onto the bed, along with the long bluish-white cord that still dangled from her, connecting her to the baby. Then Tiney placed the infant in Nette's arms. She folded a towel and laid it between her sister's legs to catch the fluids that were still seeping out.

'There's the afterbirth to deliver now, Ray,' she said. 'I'll need a large bowl. And we have to cut the cord. We need to tie it off, very firmly, and then you must cut it. But sterilise the knife in the flame first.'

Obediently, Ray fetched a reel of cotton and a clean knife and together they tied and severed the umbilical cord. A moment later, with a groan, Nette pushed out the afterbirth, a dark, bloody lump of flesh that made Ray grimace. He put his cheek against Nette's while he rested his hand on the baby's head. His eyes were shut and the concentration in his face was like that of a man in prayer. For a moment, everything in the room was as silent as a chapel. Then Ray stood up swiftly.

'I'm going for the doctor,' he said, not taking his eyes off Nette and their child as he backed towards the door. The screen door slammed behind him. Tiney heard him bounding down the steps of the hut and the truck roaring to life. A wash of relief broke over her. Help would be with them soon. She took the afterbirth away and covered the bowl with a cloth, then, tenderly, she set about cleaning Nette's legs and exchanging the damp and bloody towel for a fresh one. Finally, she pulled a fresh sheet over mother and child and then sat on the end of the bed, watching her new nephew.

Nette stroked her baby's face with her finger and the baby clamped down on it with his mouth. She unbuttoned her dress and placed the baby's small head against her breast. The stillness in the hut now that the child was born was like the calm after a storm.

Tiney made a fresh pot of tea and poured a cup for her sister. 'Will you really call him Floyd?' she asked.

'I thought I would, but he doesn't look like a Floyd, does he?' said Nette.

'Will you call him Louis, after all?'

'No,' said Nette. 'I want to call him Ray. Like his dad. Little Ray. Our ray of sunshine.' And she kissed the top of his downy head and closed her eyes.

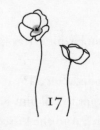

17

Dream's end

The fever came first. Tiney had just finished scrubbing the kitchen floor at Larksrest when it hit her. As she stood up, she thought she might swoon. Surely it was just the rush of blood to her head. But her throat had been throbbing all morning. She touched her neck and swallowed hard. The throbbing pain wouldn't go away. It couldn't be influenza, she thought, prayed. The epidemic had passed. She had been spared.

When Mama came back from her shopping, she took one look at Tiney and made her sit down. 'You look ghastly,' she said, placing her hand on Tiney's forehead. 'Open your mouth and stick out your tongue.'

Having inspected Tiney's tongue, Mama frowned. 'Your throat has a whitish coating and your tonsils are swollen.'

'I know,' said Tiney miserably. 'My glands are up too. I feel all hot and cold.'

'I'll fix you some soup.'

'I couldn't eat it,' said Tiney, laying her head on the cool of the scrubbed timber tabletop.

Mama sat down beside her and stroked her hair. 'I know it's been hard for you. The last bird in our family nest.' Then she put her hand against Tiney's forehead. 'You're burning up,' she said.

Mama guided Tiney into her bedroom and helped her to undress. When Tiney looked down, she saw the rash, almost like sunburn, spreading from her chest to her neck, down her torso and around to her back. There were red streaks in her armpits and elbows. When Mama touched the burning skin, her fingertips left white circles.

The doctor came and left again but Tiney had only the vaguest impression of him, of his cold hands against her brow. She saw her mother and father loom above the bed. She called out for Nette, for Minna, for Thea and then for Louis. At one stage, she felt as if she could see them all, gathered around her bed, the living and the dead. She clutched the edge of her eiderdown and tried to speak but her lips were burning, her throat parched. Then, like a dream or a miracle, Thea was there, gently tipping water between her lips.

'Thea?' she whispered, half expecting the vision of her sister to disappear.

'Mama sent me a telegram. I took the night train from Melbourne,' Thea said. But Tiney didn't know if it was now night or day or even how many days had passed since the fever had struck.

Mama and Thea took Tiney from her bed, their hands like vices around her arms, and put her in a cold bath. Her head rolled back against her will and she gasped. Then they carried her back to bed, with her matted wet hair thick around her head.

'I'm sorry, Martina.' She heard her mother's voice and the sound of shears, close to her head, snipping, as her long tresses were cut away. She could see them lying on a sheet of newspaper on the floor before Mama quickly folded the bundle of thick blond hair upon itself.

When Tiney awoke from the fever, properly woke, she felt as light as a feather. The bones of her face felt brittle, like china. The window was open and sunshine filtered into the room. Tiney raised her hand to her neck and felt its nakedness, the absence of her hair. Cautiously, she climbed out of bed. Her legs were like jelly but she felt clear in her purpose. She crossed the room, the linoleum floor cold beneath her feet, and stood before the cheval mirror. Her nightgown hung around her frame like a tent. There was so much less of her. She looked like a strange sprite. Her hair was short, and matted on the side she'd been sleeping on. She touched her ears, like two shells stuck to the side of her head. It had been so many years since she'd seen them. She had worn her hair long from when she was nine years old, and now it was gone.

Thea came into the room, carrying a tea tray. 'Tiney,' she said.

Tiney spun around, unbalanced, and made her way back to her bed where she sat down, folding her hands in her lap. 'My hair. It's gone.'

Thea put the tray down and hurried over to sit beside her, putting an arm around Tiney's shoulders and holding her close. 'I'm so sorry, Tiney. We couldn't manage it. You were sick for two weeks and it grew into an awful bird's nest, all matted and sweaty.'

'Louis loved my hair. He said I mustn't ever wear it short. Did Ma really have to cut it off?' asked Tiney.

Thea looked stricken. 'She only wanted you to be more comfortable.'

'It's all right. I don't mind,' said Tiney. 'Really I don't.

I look…modern. If you could tidy it up for me, then I might even look stylish.'

Tiney was so weak that Thea had to help her out into the back garden. She sat on a canvas chair beneath the jacaranda tree. Thea draped a towel around her shoulders and stepped back to study her profile. 'You look like a porcelain doll or a little bird. You've grown so thin, Tiney.'

Tiney glanced down at her blueish-white hands, lying in her lap.

'You've worked too hard,' said Thea as she snipped and combed Tiney's hair. 'While we've all been sad, you've been taking care of things, too many things. When you were sick, Mama and I realised just how many household tasks you had taken over. Tiney, it was too much for you. You're barely eighteen!'

'Am I? Did I miss my birthday?'

'Yes, darling. You did. And Armistice Day's anniversary too. It's more than a year now since the war ended.'

'I'm sorry,' said Tiney.

'What are you apologising for?' asked Thea.

'For disappointing you.'

'Stop it. Now you're being ridiculous. You didn't disappoint anyone. But you need to take care of yourself and you need a holiday. Paul's coming on Friday to take you up to Nuriootpa.'

'No!' said Tiney. 'I promised Nette I'd go back to Cobdogla and help with baby Ray. I have to, as soon as I'm strong enough. And who's going to help Mama take care of Papa? I haven't time for a holiday.'

Thea laid down her scissors and knelt in front of her little sister. 'Tiney, we nearly lost you. How could we bear it? You are too precious, to all of us, to risk losing. I'm going to stay home and help Mama. We will be all right. We want you to get better. In the Barossa, you can simply rest. You won't have to do anything at all and the country air will be good for you. Onkel Ludwig and Tante Bea have offered to have you stay with them for as long as you need.'

Tiney began to cry, though she quickly realised the tears were a mixture of relief and frustration. A flurry of petals drifted down from the jacaranda tree and landed on her skirt. As she brushed them from her lap, she thought of how a whole year had slipped by since she had stood under the jacaranda tree listening to the church bells of Adelaide ringing in peace. Her dreams felt as broken as the possibility of love.

18

Barossa

Paul held out his hand to help Tiney down from Onkel Ludwig's car. For a moment, she felt like a girl from a cinema poster, standing on the running board of a Studebaker in her new dress with the tips of her sharply cut blonde bob peeping out from beneath a cloche hat.

Onkel Ludwig and Tante Bea's home, Vogelsang, was a house of nooks and crannies, of gabled windows and intricate fretwork. It had five chimneys and a long return verandah that wrapped around the red-brick and sandstone walls. Tante Bea welcomed Tiney, and Paul carried her suitcase into the cool of the bedroom. Exhausted from the journey, she sat in the window seat, overlooking the garden. It was dry and sandy in comparison to Larksrest with low shrubs and a stand of gums near the new paling fence.

Tiney watched as Paul crossed the driveway and collected his bicycle from the garage. He wheeled it out into the street, swung a leg over the seat and pedalled off to his job at the chemist's shop. Then Onkel drove off in the Studebaker to visit his vine-yards. Tiney lay down on the bed and stared at the ceiling. In the distance a magpie sang, but inside Vogelsang all sounds were muffled. She shut her eyes and slept.

When she woke, she found someone had come into her room and unpacked her things. Her books and letter-writing folio were neatly arranged on the dresser. Tiney flipped open the folio and took out the photograph of Louis to prop beside her bed, alongside the family photo of her parents and sisters. She felt a twinge of guilt as she rearranged the remaining photos and papers. The night before, she had crept into Papa's study and rifled through his desk drawer to find the photo of the mysterious woman and child. Papa claimed he had read through Louis' diary and carefully reviewed all his letters but could find no mention of anyone like them. He disdained putting the photograph in his precious scrapbook of Louis' life. What if the woman in the photo was really a person of no consequence, someone who had no true connection to Louis? Was there ever any way of knowing what she had meant to him? Tiney put the photo in an envelope and tucked it into the back of her writing folio.

The days fell into an easy rhythm. Tiney spent much of them sleeping. It was as if all the restless nights of the past year had caught up with her, for within an hour of breakfast she had so little energy that simply getting dressed and eating left her exhausted. All she could do was creep back to her room and lie down again until the bell rang for lunch.

Tante Bea wanted no help from Tiney, despite her frequent complaints about needing a daughter. Two girls came every morning to sweep and dust and to boil the big copper kettle in the back laundry. They helped Tante Bea in her endless rounds of pickling and preserving. They brought in the spring harvest from the kitchen garden and the orchard, and peeled and chopped, salted vegetables and stewed fruit to fill shining glass jars while Tiney sat reading on the return verandah, saving her energy for the evenings.

Dinners at Vogelsang were much more formal than at Larksrest. Tiney missed the chatter of her sisters and the easy tenderness between her parents, though she took pleasure in the easy way everyone spoke German here, without Nette to scold. Though her uncle and aunt sometimes smiled at her mistakes, she was grateful for their patience and unstinting kindness. Tiney felt as if the most important way she could repay her uncle and aunt was to make them laugh. She had the feeling that no one had laughed at Vogelsang for a very long time.

When the table was cleared, Tiney and Paul sat at the piano together and played duets. It was soothing to have music to cover the terrible silences between Paul and his parents. Paul was a much more accomplished musician than Tiney, and she loved sitting beside him watching his hands racing up and down the ivory keys. He also had a beautiful baritone voice and when he sang Schumann's Dichterliebe song cycle, Onkel Ludwig would grow teary. Tante Bea would hand him her handkerchief, which always made Tiney smile.

But by far the best part of the day, as far as Tiney was concerned, was when Paul came cycling up the driveway in the late afternoon. Tiney would try to make sure she was in the garden when he arrived so they could talk without Tante Bea listening to every word. In the presence of his parents, Paul's face closed over like a darkening sky, but when it was just the two of them, he would tell her stories and jokes to make her laugh, and tease her affectionately. It made him seem more like his brother Will. It made her want to trust him.

It was while they were sitting beneath a plum tree in the orchard on a December evening, eating the first blood-red fruit of the season, that Tiney showed him the photo. Paul wiped his hands on the yellow grass and took it from her carefully.

'It was in Louis' things that were sent from the Front. Mama and Papa won't let us talk about it but I can't help wondering if this could be Louis' child,' said Tiney, leaning forward and pointing to the baby.

'It could be anyone's son,' he said dismissively, handing the picture back to Tiney.

'Do you think it's a boy? I really couldn't tell. But why would he keep the photo? It must be someone he knew well. And the woman is very pretty, don't you think?'

'For a Jewess, I suppose she is,' said Paul. He stretched out in the long grass and stared up at the summer sky.

'Now you're teasing me. You can't know she's a Jew,' said Tiney. 'You're simply guessing. We can't know anything about them and we probably never will. She belongs to a different world.'

'Yes, the real world,' said Paul, bitterly.

'It's no more real than here,' said Tiney.

A murder of black crows flew over the orchard and wheeled towards the river. The silence between Paul and Tiney stretched out like a chill wind.

'Do you feel strong enough for a stroll?' asked Paul suddenly. 'Or we could take the car and go for a drive, if you don't feel like walking.'

'Why don't we do both?' said Tiney. 'Let's drive and then walk. You keep telling me you're going to show me all the magical places in the Barossa. It's about time I got the Paul Kreiger tour.'

Paul smiled. 'So you're feeling brave, little cousin?'

'I always feel brave,' replied Tiney.

They drove through Nuriootpa, past an old cemetery and along a dusty track. The sky was splashed with coppery clouds but the evening was warm and there were still many hours before darkness. After driving through valleys green with grapevines and over dusky golden hills, they parked beside a towering, white-barked gum tree.

'So, my courageous cousin, are you ready to face the black heart of the Barossa? Do you know that a *Zauberer*, a sorcerer, fought the devil not very far from here?'

Tiney laughed.

'No, it's true. My father used to scare me and Will when we went hiking here as boys. The end of the world was nigh and the *Zauberer* fought the devil to save us all.'

'On Mount Kitchener?' asked Tiney.

'You know it's not Mount Kitchener,' said Paul, his tone changing. 'It's Kaiserstuhl – the Emperor's seat. Sixty-nine names from the map of South Australia have been changed this year. Sixty-nine! Even poor little Schuber is now Stuart. Ridiculous.'

Tiney sighed. 'Let's not fight, Paul. I'm sorry. I wasn't thinking. Nette insisted on using the British names, you know that.'

'How can you listen to her?'

'Because she's my big sister and I love her. But I don't want to argue with you. Tell me about the sorcerer and the end of the world.'

'Have you heard of old Kavel, the Lutheran minister who brought out hundreds of Germans back in 1838? Your mother used to hear him preach when she was growing up in Tanunda. Some say he was the sorcerer in this story. Kavel was always predicting the end of days. Some say he practised grey magic, others say that's rubbish. Perhaps it was someone else. Who knows? When our people left their old homes, they brought more than themselves to this country.'

'But for us, it's different, isn't it?' asked Tiney. 'We were born here, you and me. We're part of the new country, not the old.'

Paul shrugged. 'Do you want to hear the story or not?'

Tiney nodded and Paul's voice dropped into storytelling mode.

'So this old *Zauberer*, this man of grey magic, he brought his powers with him from Germany. And when he came here, to this place and saw the mountain and the ravine, he knew that when the devil was about to ascend to the world it would be from Kaiserstuhl Mountain. He also knew that when the devil came, he would transform himself into the red-bearded troll, Barbarossa.

'So the *Zauberer* ordered the blacksmith down in Nuriootpa to make chains so strong they could bind the Devil. Then the citizens shored up the sides of Tanunda jail in preparation for his capture.'

'Why?'

'For when the *Zauberer* succeeded, of course, and came down the mountain with the Devil in tow. Eight men dragged chains up steep roads, with the *Zauberer* leading the way. It was the blackest night of the century. Some say they came back down the next morning shamefaced. But there is another story about what happened on that dark night.'

Paul opened the car door and jumped out, striding up the path ahead. Tiney ran after him, catching his arm. 'You can't leave off there!' she said, breathlessly, trying to keep pace with him.

Paul grinned. 'Some say that the *Zauberer* and his apprentices climbed the mountain in a wind so strong they could barely stand. Then blue lightning struck the chains and...' Paul clapped his hands loudly and Tiney jumped. 'The apprentices were vaporised. But the *Zauberer* stood his ground. All night, he fought from inside a *Hexenkreis* that he'd drawn on the ground with the charred leg-bone of an apprentice. And he read from a *Zauberbuch*, his magical book of sorcery. At dawn, when the *Zauberer* came back down to Tanunda, he was scorched black.'

'Did he have the Devil with him?' asked Tiney

'Well, the people of the town asked him whether he had caught the Devil. He told them he had chained the beast and cast it into the devil-pit at the foot of Kaiserstuhl.'

Tiney glanced around the bush uneasily.

'So the Devil is beneath the ground, right here in the Barossa?'

Paul shrugged. 'If you try hard enough, you can imagine it's true.'

Tiney tried to picture the sorcerer with his face scorched black. All she could conjure was exactly what she saw – Paul, gazing broodingly over the landscape.

Paul raised his hand and pointed upwards. 'That gorge, over there, that's where the Devil stays chained.' He grabbed a broken branch and began bashing his way through the long grass and scrub towards the fissure in the rock. Tiney followed. When they reached it, they stood and stared at the deep, black opening in the stone.

'It's just a story,' said Paul. 'There's nothing there. There's nothing here at all. They try and mix the old stories with this place and it doesn't work. You can tell it has its own stories – ones that we don't know, stories that don't belong to me just as I don't belong here.'

'I can imagine the Devil crawling out of the darkness here,' said Tiney.

'No,' said Paul. 'The Devil has been too busy on the other side of the world.' Paul dropped the branch and slumped onto his knees.

Tiney put her hand on his shoulder. 'What's wrong, Paul?'

Paul's shoulders rose and fell, as if he was gasping. 'I need to leave, Tiney. I need to leave the Barossa.'

'But this is your home. You were born here, grew up here.'

'I have these other places in my head. It doesn't work, to lock the old gods up in this place, the old stories. They don't fit and I don't fit either. I can't get Germany out of my mind or out of my soul.'

'You've never even been there,' said Tiney.

'That doesn't change how I feel. I keep thinking of Will. I think of what he went through. It could have been both of us. I was only a year off following him to Heidelberg.'

'I'm glad you didn't go,' said Tiney.

Paul turned his face away from her. 'If I had gone, maybe it would have been me, not Will, who died. He might have come home.'

'You mustn't even think that, Paul.'

'You don't understand!' he cried.

'But I do! I do understand. Grief can make you think mad thoughts. When Louis died, it was as if a big black hole opened up and swallowed all my family and we broke into tiny little pieces as we fell into it. I had a dream, that if we could all go to Europe together, me and Mama and Papa and all my sisters, then somehow we would be made whole. But I couldn't make it come true. Everyone kept breaking away – first Nette, then Minna and finally Thea. And Mama and Papa, they've grown so much older in only a year. Then I fell ill. And that was the end of it all.'

'You could still go,' said Paul, his eyes feverishly bright. 'We could go together. My trust money could pay for both of us. We wouldn't have to come back here, ever.'

Tiney felt faint. The sun was low on the western horizon and sunlight cut through the leaves of the trees, blinding her.

'I only wanted to go for a visit, Paul, not forever! You're all Tante and Onkel have left. It would break their hearts if you left them. They've already lost one son. They mustn't lose another.'

Paul scuffed the ground with the tip of his shiny black boot. A shroud of golden dust coated the leather.

'So you won't come with me?'

'To France?'

'No, to Germany.'

'But it's not safe in Germany, not even to visit. Haven't you read about the terrible revolutionaries and riots? You know Rosa Luxemburg and Karl Liebnecht were murdered, and other socialists too! And what if the Russian civil war spills over? You're lucky you weren't extradited with the other German prisoners. You're lucky that you're really Australian.'

'They should have extradited me instead of half the good men they've sent back. Some of them were more Australian than I will ever be. I wish I was with them. They arrived back in Germany in September. They're building a new Europe and here I am, like a child, playing in the bush with my baby cousin.'

Paul thrust his hands into his pockets. Tiney leapt to her feet, and stood squarely facing Paul with her hands on her hips. 'I am not a baby, Paul. One day, I'll find where Louis is buried. And maybe Will too. But then I'll come home and help build *this* country.'

Paul said nothing and they walked in stormy silence back to the car. By the time they reached Vogelsang, darkness had fallen. Tiney went to her room and lay on her bed, her mind as thunderous as the night the *Zauberer* fought the devil.

19

Ready to fly

Tiney dreamt of Louis. He was running towards her across a field of poppies. Her heart soared at the sight of him. A breeze made the poppies sway and the long grass parted before him as he ran. Tiney wanted to run to meet him but her body wouldn't cooperate. He was almost next to her when the bombs began to fall. The field of flowers turned to sludge, Louis stumbled, and his hands fell heavily on her shoulders, dragging her downwards as he sank into grey mud. She turned to look into his face, but it was the face of a stranger.

Someone was shaking Tiney, with firm hands on each of her shoulders. When Tiney finally managed to drag herself from her nightmare, she realised it was Tante Bea, and she was crying.

'Tante,' said Tiney. 'What's wrong, what's happened?'

'Paulie,' said Tante Bea. 'I know there was something not right between you. Did you have a fight yesterday?'

'We did disagree about Kaiserstuhl being called Mount Kitchener,' said Tiney, guiltily, not wanting to tell Tante Bea everything.

'Paul has gone. Packed his bags and run away.'

'Run away?'

'We know he has had letters. From Germany. From someone he met while he was interned. They have tricked him, lured him from us. First we have lost one son to the war and now we will lose the other.' Tante Bea sat on the end of the bed and the tears flooded down her cheeks.

'Did he leave a note for you, Tante?' asked Tiney, one hand over her aunt's. 'Didn't he say why he's gone?'

'No, not a note. What did he say to you?'

'I told him I wanted to go and find where Louis was buried and he said he wanted to go to Europe too.'

'You really want to do this thing?' asked Tante Bea. 'To travel all that way to visit a grave?'

'Yes. One day,' said Tiney. 'Maybe Paul wants to visit Will's grave too. He misses him very much.'

Tante Bea hugged Tiney. 'You are a good girl. You think of your family. Not like Paul. He is not searching for Will for us. Paul only does things for Paul.'

'He means well, Tante,' said Tiney.

Tante Bea covered her face with her hands. 'Paul is not a good boy, but he is all we have left, Martina.' Then she began to cry again, her mouth turned down like an inverted 'U', her face stony even as tears streamed down her cheeks.

Tiney climbed out of bed and drew the curtains. The day outside was bright and soft, full of the promise of a summer morning. For the first time in weeks, Tiney felt the stirrings of her old strength.

'Tante Bea,' she said, turning to her aunt. 'If we can get to Adelaide by this evening, we might be able to find Paul. He must be somewhere in town.'

Tante Bea stopped sobbing and looked at Tiney.

'Where would we begin?'

'The train station, the docks, the coffee palaces, the hotels. He might have contacted Thea. We might be able to stop him.'

After breakfast, Tiney quickly packed her suitcase and tidied her bedroom. Onkel Ludwig was already backing the Studebaker out of the garage for the drive to Adelaide.

When Tiney picked up her letter-writing folio to add to her suitcase, she noticed the stationery was untidily stuffed into the cover. Someone had been rifling through it. The blue envelopes had been hastily pushed back into the inside pocket and the small collection of photos that she kept in the back of the folio had been crammed in a jumble between folds of vellum stationery. Sorting through them methodically, she discovered one was missing: Louis' photo of the woman and the baby.

Quietly, Tiney pushed open the door to Paul's room. Though nothing was out of place, the room felt abandoned, or perhaps, Paul had never really settled back into it. The pale blue chenille coverlet on his bed lay smooth and unruffled. Tiney stood beside the bedside table, looking at the cover of the last book that Paul had been reading. It was a collection of Goethe's poems. She touched the green cover lightly. A gum leaf lay wedged between two pages and she flipped the book open to see which poem he'd bookmarked. Three lines in German were underlined:

No one ought to refuse to receive what is offer'd with liberal kindness.
No one can tell how long he will keep what in peace he possesses,
No one, how long he is doom'd in foreign countries to wander…

She shut the book.

Tiney sat between her aunt and uncle on the long drive through the hills, down to Adelaide.

'Paul was seen riding on his bicycle towards Tanunda not long after nine o'clock last night,' said Onkel Ludwig. 'He may be leaving Adelaide now. It may be too late to find him.'

'He might have been to see Thea first,' said Tiney.

Tante Bea shook her head. 'You were his favourite, Tiney. If he could leave without telling you, then he won't be speaking to your sister.'

Tiney hung her head, confused and with a nagging sense of guilt. Had their argument triggered Paul's departure? And why had he taken the photo of the woman and child? What could it possibly mean to him?

'Did he say anything to you about his plans?' asked Onkel Ludwig.

'I told him that I wanted to go to France to visit Louis' grave and Paul said he wanted to go to Germany. But it was only talk.'

'What talk is this of visiting graves?' said Onkel Ludwig, his pale eyes serious as his gaze flicked between the road and Tiney's face.

Tiney picked at her sleeve as she told her aunt and uncle about the Alstons' plans to visit Charlie's grave, about her longing to find Louis' grave too, with her family. When she'd finished, she looked up to see her uncle and aunt glancing at each other over the top of her head. She sank a little lower in her seat and stared at the long road through the hills.

When they reached Adelaide, they went straight to Larksrest but the look of surprise on Thea's face as she opened the front door made it clear they hadn't heard from Paul.

Tante Bea stayed talking to Thea and Mama while Tiney

and Onkel Ludwig set out for the railway station. A train had left for Western Australia that morning but the stationmaster made enquiries for them and said no one of Paul's description had bought a ticket. At Port Adelaide, Onkel Ludwig found out that the *Morea* had sailed at dawn. At the ticket office, they were told a young man named Kreiger had bought a berth in steerage just before midnight. Paul was gone.

Mama and Tante Bea were sitting at the table in the kitchen at Larksrest, ready with tea and seed cake, waiting for their return. Tiney saw Tante Bea visibly slump when they walked into the room without Paul. She left Onkel Ludwig to break the bad news and went to her room to unpack. Thea was sitting on the end of her bed but she leapt up and hugged Tiney tightly.

'I'm so glad to have you home,' said Thea. 'I was going to write to you but it's much better you're here.' She crossed the room and opened a drawer in her dresser. 'Close your eyes.'

Puzzled, Tiney obeyed.

'Put out your hands,' said Thea.

Tiney felt something cool and round in her left hand and a thick wad of paper being placed in her right. 'Now open!' said Thea.

Tiney looked down to see a shining gold medal in one hand and an envelope in the other.

'The medal is just for you to look at it,' said Thea, smiling. 'But the envelope is yours to keep.'

Tiney looked at the medal first. It bore an image of a Grecian woman holding an easel and palm frond – the symbol of the South Australian Society of Arts. 'You won!' she shouted. She flung her arms around Thea. 'I thought you'd withdrawn your picture from the competition.'

'I did. Then I entered another painting of Christie's Beach in its place. But don't forget the envelope. What's inside it is just for you.'

Tiney hurriedly flipped it open and then caught her breath. Inside was a stack of crisp ten-pound notes.

'The prize money,' said Thea. 'It's not enough for a fare to England, but it will help with other things when you go away.'

'Away?' asked Tiney. 'Oh Thea, I'm never going to be able to save the rest of the fare. You think too much of me.'

Thea smiled. 'And you think too little of yourself. What I know is that your ears should have been burning all afternoon. Mama and Tante Bea have been talking about you nonstop.'

Tiney felt a shiver go up her spine, as if her body understood what her sister was hinting at even as she gazed at Thea in bewilderment.

When she walked back into the kitchen, Papa was sitting there too, looking hollow and sad. But when he saw Tiney, he smiled. Onkel put both his plump hands on the table, as if he were about to make a speech. He drew breath, stroked his beard, and then looked at Tante Bea, not Tiney, as he spoke.

'Your Mama and Papa and your Onkel and Tante have been speaking of you, Tiney. We have, together, made a plan. Your Tante and I will be paying your passage to Europe, as long as the Alstons are happy to accompany you.'

Tiney clapped her hands to her face in surprise.

'We ask one small favour in exchange,' continued Onkel Ludwig. 'When you are visiting the Western Front with the Alstons, we would like for you to make an enquiry on our behalf. We would like to know where our Wilhelm rests. For us, two German-Australians seeking their dead German son, it would be too difficult; we know the Red Cross struggles with these requests and the correspondence, it takes years. But perhaps, if you are in Europe, you will find a way. If Paul has tried doing this also, perhaps you will hear news of him. This is a very large thing to ask of you, but rest assured we do not expect you to do more than enquire on our behalf.'

Tiney couldn't speak. Her guilt at arguing with Paul, perhaps precipitating his departure, left her tongue-tied.

Tante Bea stood up and reached for Tiney's hand. 'Tiney, we are too old to make this journey ourselves. If it is only lack of money that has stopped you, then we are more than willing to help. We want to honour our dear nephew Louis, but your journey could be for all of us, for all our boys. For Louis, for Wilhelm, and for Paul whom we have lost as well, though not to God.'

'Perhaps she's not strong enough,' said Papa. 'She's only a girl, our Tiney.'

'Are you strong enough for this, Martina?' asked Tante Bea.

Tiney took both her aunt's hands and held them tight. Then she smiled.

'I'm more than strong, Tante. I'm ready.'

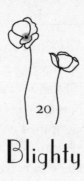

20

Blighty

Tiney checked the clasp on her red enamel brooch and straight-ened the little red sail as she stood on the upper deck of the *Orvieto*. Then she crossed to the railing and stared down into the milling crowds on the dock. All the Flynns, along with Paul's parents, stood in a cluster, holding down their hats against the wind whipping off the sea. Tiney raised both her hands and waved, hoping they could pick her out from the hundreds of passengers hanging over the rails of the ocean liner.

It felt wrong to be leaving all her sisters behind and setting out into the world alone. The one compensation was that at least her journey had brought her family together. They hadn't all been able to gather in Adelaide for Christmas but everyone had been at Larksrest on New Year's Eve, in time to see Tiney before she left with the Alstons on the second of January. Minna and Frank had caught the train from Melbourne, and Nette and Ray had come down from Cobdolga with baby Ray.

Ida came along the deck and slipped one arm around Tiney's shoulders.

'I'm so glad you're with us,' she said, pressing a roll of blue paper streamers into Tiney's hand. 'I know I'm not a real sister but perhaps we can pretend I'm the fifth Flynn girl. Can you see the family down there in the crowd?'

'Yes, but I don't think they can see me,' said Tiney.

'We'll fix that.' Ida drew back her arm and threw her roll of streamers high into the air. It arced out over the top of the crowd, a rippling red ribbon. Tiney wrapped one end of her streamer around her wrist and flung it to the wind. The blue streamer tangled with the red and drifted down to the crowd.

Thea was the first to look up and see where Tiney and Ida stood waving. She raised both her arms. Nette held up baby Ray's tiny plump arm and waved it in the air too. Suddenly, the whole party of Flynns, Kriegers, Stauntons and McCaffreys raised their arms. Tiney laughed through her tears.

The first night out, as they sailed across the Bight, Tiney was horribly seasick; but by the time they left Fremantle she had found her sea legs. In the early morning, she crept out of the cabin she shared with Ida and made her way up on deck to watch the last sliver of Australian coastline disappear into a blue haze.

Some days, as they sailed north and heat washed over the deck, Tiney felt as though she was floating between her old life and the next, only half alive, as if part of her spirit had slipped away when her sisters had vanished from sight on the docks of Port Adelaide. The ship called at Durban and Capetown and then sailed up the coast of Africa. Then they went along the Suez Canal, past Port Said, gold and amber in the evening light, and finally across the Mediterranean Sea.

Marseilles was Tiney's first sight of Europe. She stood on the deck, leaning over the rails in the cool morning. Swarthy men drenched in sunlight milled upon the dock, and beyond them, cobbled streets stretched into the township. Marseilles smelt of ships and oil, of men and fish and a dozen other scents she couldn't name. Somewhere, hundreds of miles to the north, Louis lay buried beneath the soil of this country. She wanted to run down the gangplank to touch the earth, as if that would magically connect her to her brother.

When the ship finally landed at Plymouth, Mrs Alston let out a sigh of relief. 'Home at last,' she said, as the gangplanks were lowered.

The train from Plymouth to London sped through green fields beneath a soft blue sky. Everything was muted and somehow both more and less than Tiney had expected of England. It didn't feel like 'home' to her. She thought of the rocky Burren in Ireland that her father's family had come from, she imagined the banks of the Rhine in Germany from where her great-grandparents had left to come to Australia, but neither tugged at her heartstrings. Only Larksrest would ever be home. Yet stepping from the railway carriage onto the platform at Paddington Station was like walking into the pages of every British storybook Tiney had ever read. The bustling crowds in dark clothing, the light filtering through the cavernous glass ceiling, the white steam from the engines in the chill air – every image conjured a hundred possibilities of adventure.

Mrs Alston had taken rooms near Hyde Park and Ida organised a taxicab. Self-consciously, Tiney added her single cardboard suitcase to the Alstons' huge pile of trunks.

Ida and Tiney's room was a small second-floor bedroom overlooking the street. Tiney stood by the window and looked out at the streetscape. It was only four o'clock but already the sky was growing dark. Ida began unpacking her trunk but she couldn't reach the wardrobe without dancing awkwardly around Tiney.

'This is worse than our cabin!' she exclaimed. 'What was Mummy thinking, to book such teeny-weeny digs? You sit on the bed while I unpack and then you can have your turn.'

Tiney tucked her feet underneath the covers to keep warm. 'I think we'll be going for a lot of walks in the next month, if only to be out of this cubby,' she said.

'Don't worry, old chum,' Ida laughed. 'We're going to the South Downs at the weekend. Mummy's cousin, Mrs Bertha Bloomfield, has a gorgeous house down there. White cliffs and all that. We'd smother each other if we had to be locked up here for more than a few days.'

Tiney's heart sank a little at the thought of more travel. This was what she'd prayed for, but now, in this small, cold room in London, she could only think of the sunlight streaming in through her bedroom window at Larksrest.

Mrs Alston fussed all through dinner. 'Florence Finton recommended Mrs Greenleigh's very highly and I thought it would be nice for us to be somewhere homey,' she said in a whisper. 'But perhaps we should move to a hotel.'

'I only just unpacked, Mummy,' said Ida. 'And besides, Tiney and I have so much sightseeing to do, we can't possibly move tomorrow.'

Ida was up first the next morning, bathed and ready for the day before Tiney had even woken. 'Mummy says she wants to spend the whole day resting,' said Ida. 'But you and I are going to take London by storm.'

She handed Tiney a cup of steaming, milky tea. Tiney sat up, pushed aside the curtain and peeped out at the street again as she cradled the fine china cup in her hands. Everything outside was still grey despite the thin morning light.

As they stepped out into the street, Tiney wrapped her woollen scarf tightly around her neck and tucked it into the collar of her plain brown jacket. Ida pulled on her pea-green coat with the rabbit fur collar and together, like a sparrow and a bird of paradise, they headed out into the chill London morning. Clusters of snowdrops pushed up in tiny front gardens, the first hint that spring was not far away.

When they finally reached Whitehall, the day had grown brighter. The Cenotaph stood in the middle of the road on its own small concrete island between the Foreign Office and Richmond House. It was a tall pylon that looked as though it was made of stone, looming grey against a pale grey sky. Tiney knew it was only constructed of wood and plaster, hurriedly built for last year's Peace Day celebrations, but it was still impressive. Carved laurel wreaths decorated both sides and a third laurel wreath rested on top. Dozens of floral tributes, some faded, some fresh, lay piled on the steps around the base. Women were milling around the memorial, most of them middle-aged or elderly, dressed in dark coats. One woman had a little boy with her, clutching a small bouquet of violets exactly the same as the one Tiney had bought from a roadside flower-seller. Tiney knelt down and laid her violets beside a simple posy of asters that someone had tucked between the more sombre offerings.

Beside her, an old woman was struggling to raise herself from her knees. Tiney helped her to her feet.

'Thank you,' the woman said, straightening herself. 'I come

here every Tuesday but I'm not getting any younger. I want to keep coming until I see them set it right. Sir Edwin Luytens, the architect, he's got them making a permanent Cenotaph of real stone so it will be with us forever.'

'We've come all the way from Australia to see it,' said Tiney.

'Oh, the Australians! The Australians were marching here on Peace Day in July last year, when they unveiled the Cenotaph,' said the old woman. 'People stayed up all night – thousands of us, camping out anywhere so we wouldn't miss the parade. Everyone was showering your diggers with gifts – fruit, cigarettes, flowers. There was so much gratitude, so much heartfelt gratitude.' She patted Tiney's hand and tottered across the road towards the bus stop.

'So many women feeling grateful to our boys,' said Ida, scanning the crowd. 'You know, there's not a single man among them. It makes you think, doesn't it?'

'Think what?' asked Tiney.

'That we're all doomed to spinsterhood. They say there are two million "excess women" here in Britain, and they're encouraging young ones to migrate to the Dominions to find husbands. As if we need any more competition!'

'Oh, Ida!' said Tiney. 'We're meant to be thinking about grief, not boyfriends. I think it's all terribly poignant but awfully depressing.'

Ida looked at her in surprise. 'If the Cenotaph upsets you, how much worse will it be when we visit the boys' graves? How will you cope?'

'I'm not upset,' said Tiney, trying to think how to explain herself. 'That old lady comes here every day to this empty tomb. Every day! I want to see where Louis is buried but I don't want to spend the rest of my life dwelling on his death. He wrote so many letters from London. He wrote about walking in Hyde Park and Trafalgar Square and visiting St Paul's Cathedral and Piccadilly Circus at night. There were so many places that he visited when he came to "Blighty". While we're in England, I'd like to open a little window onto his life. He died in France, not here. We'll see the graves soon enough. Before then, I want to see how he lived. All those things he wrote about will feel more real if I can see them too.'

Ida suddenly laughed. 'I like the way you think, Tiney Flynn. Charlie came to London twice and loved it, and Daddy was born here, so I have a lot to explore too. Let's live a little.' She hooked one arm through Tiney's and they made their way out into the London traffic.

21

On Beachy Head

The Alstons' elderly cousin Mrs Bloomfield lived in a Tudor house with a perfectly kept garden a few miles from Newhaven in Sussex. She'd lost both her sons and her husband in the war, so was glad to have the company of Australian relatives. Their first week in Sussex was grey and cold, but one morning they woke to a perfect spring day. Ida announced they should attempt a picnic somewhere on the South Downs and volunteered to drive the big black Bentley.

'Take care, Ida!' said Mrs Alston, as the car bounced down a tiny country road.

In some places, hedgerows rose up high on either side of the road, blocking the view. Tiney leaned out the window, taking in lungfuls of fresh air. Ida turned the Bentley onto a cart road and bumped through a field to reach a hilltop overlooking the sea.

The younger women lifted the picnic baskets out of the boot while Mrs Alston helped Mrs Bloomfield out of the car. Then Ida took charge and determinedly guided everyone along the track. They tramped up the hillside to the edge of the cliffs where they spread picnic rugs on the ground in a spot sheltered from the wind. From the cliff tops of Beachy Head they could see right across the English Channel.

Ida unpacked their lunch – cold pork pies, a little jar of chutney, some bread and cheese, apples and a big bottle of ginger beer. It was almost too cold to enjoy the picnic, despite the spring sunshine. While the others drank hot tea from a thermos to warm up, Tiney wandered to the edge of the white, chalky cliffs and looked out to sea. A red and white lighthouse stood in the silvery-green water. On the other side of the lighthouse, across the English Channel, beyond the mists, lay France.

Further along the edge of the cliffs, Tiney noticed a man, standing no more than fifty yards from her, staring out over the water. There was something about the set of his body that reminded her of Sebastian Farr. Even at a distance, Tiney could see he was tall and lanky with strong, chiselled features. She turned and ran back to Ida. 'Do you think that man, the one over there, do you think he's all right?'

'A lot of them come up here to finish themselves off, ' said Mrs Bloomfield. 'The ones that can't cope. Some of them make such a terrible mess when they hit the rocks below that no one can establish their identity.'

'Bertha!' admonished Mrs Alston. 'What a ghastly thing to say.'

But Tiney didn't hear Mrs Alston's scolding. She had already jumped to her feet and was racing along the cliff top, towards the man. He hadn't moved. As Tiney ran she imagined what must lie behind his eyes as he stared at the misty horizon. She called out to him, 'Sir! Please, sir!'

The stranger turned to look at her and, instantly, Tiney realised her mistake. She stopped in her tracks, blushing.

'I just thought...I mean, I imagined...' She was too embarrassed to confess.

The man laughed. 'It was very good of you,' he said. 'But I'm far too selfish to need saving.'

Tiney raised one hand to shade her eyes as she looked up at him. His thick black hair was cropped short and his eyes were deep-set in a gaunt, gypsy face. 'I didn't think I was that obvious. Are you a mind-reader?' she asked.

'Only of good-hearted souls,' he replied. 'Do you often go patrolling the white cliffs, hoping to save lonely men from themselves?'

'No,' said Tiney. 'But I would. I mean, I wouldn't like to see anyone lose hope. "*He who goes lonely comes not back again...*"'

'That's by the Australian poet Mary Gilmore, isn't it?'

Tiney was speechless with embarrassment. Why had she thought to quote a poem at this man? 'I didn't think it was very well known, outside Australia,' she said

'"*But these, these fellowing men, shall know
Love's memory though they go*,"' said the stranger, quoting the last line of the stanza. Then he laughed. 'I'm from Australia.'

'You don't sound very Australian,' said Tiney.

'I'm from Victor Harbor. I served with the Eleventh Field Ambulance, Australian Third Division. I was demobilised last year but I've stayed on to do other work.'

'My sister was in the Eleventh Field Ambulance Ladies Sewing Circle.'

'I presume you're from Adelaide, then.'

'Yes,' said Tiney. 'And so are my friends over there. I'm Martina Flynn.'

'It seems we're two of a kind. I'm Martin Woolf,' he said.

'You know our names – Martina and Martin – mean "warlike".'

'I'm not warlike at all. My friends call me Tiney.'

'Then I hope you'll allow me that privilege,' he said. He offered his hand to Tiney, and she felt warmth radiate up her arm.

'Your hands are icy cold,' he said with surprise, and he placed his other hand over Tiney's small one. 'Let me walk you back to your companions. It's easy to twist an ankle on this rough ground.'

'I won't fall, and even if I did I'm much closer to the ground than most people, so I never hurt myself,' said Tiney as they walked back along the cliff.

Martin smiled. 'Unbreakable, are you?'

'No, but I'm hardier than I look. I'm on my way to France, to visit the grave of my brother.'

Martin's expression changed and he stopped in his tracks. 'Civilians aren't allowed on the battlefields.'

'We're not ordinary civilians, not tourists. We're more like pilgrims.'

'And where exactly are you headed to on this pilgrimage?'

'Villers-Bretonneux and then a place called the Buire British Cemetery. Though I'm still not exactly sure where that is. I believe it's somewhere between Tincourt and Péronne.'

Martin glanced out to sea and then back at Tiney. 'The cemeteries aren't ready for mourners, not yet.'

Tiney looked up into his dark brown eyes and measured her words before she spoke.

'I may be small and not very old, but I'm not naive. I have no illusions that I may witness terrible things. But my brother saw far worse and I will not spare myself his pain. I want to honour his death.'

'You can only honour the dead by living.'

Tiney heard Ida's voice, carried on the sea breeze. She turned and saw her companions had already packed up the picnic rug and Ida was waving for her to join them.

'I must go,' said Tiney. 'I'm glad you weren't in need of rescue.'

Martin offered her his arm and together they walked back, awkwardly silent, to the Alstons' car. Martin Woolf introduced himself politely to everyone and helped load the picnic basket into the boot. As Tiney leaned out the car window to say good-bye, Martin spoke first.

'I believe I may be able to help you, Miss Flynn. I was stationed at Villers-Bretonneux and briefly at Bois de Buire near Tincourt. I could draw you a sketch of how to find Buire-Courcelles, which is where the British Cemetery is located, and some details of people who may be able to help you at Villers-Bretonneux.'

Ida leaned across the front seat. 'Too kind of you, Mr Woolf,' she said. 'We'll be at Mrs Bloomfield's, on the Lewes road from Seaford. If you could pop something in the post, that would be spiffing.'

Martin stepped away from the car and waved goodbye. Tiney watched his figure disappear as the car turned onto the country road and the hedgerows blocked him from view.

'Mr Woolf!' said Ida. She nudged Tiney and winked. 'Did you ask him for the time?'

'Don't tease, Ida,' said Tiney. 'We could have at least invited him to call on us. He could have been really helpful. You were awful telling him to "pop it in the post".'

'Well, he has the choice of posting something or coming to call, now he knows where we are. But I'm your chaperone, darling Little Red Riding Hood. It's my job to save you from tall, dark and handsome strangers.'

She revved the engine and the car sped up over a rise. In the back seat, Mrs Bloomfield and Mrs Alston gasped. Tiney held onto her seat and smiled to herself.

22

Love's memory

They took the ferry from Folkestone on a windy spring morning. Mrs Alston was sick much of the way and by the time they reached Calais she was exhausted. Tiney and Ida helped her off the ferry and found a car to take them to the nearest hotel. Luckily, Ida had been persuaded to leave most of her luggage with Mrs Bloomfield.

The next morning, they took the train to Amiens and from there went direct to Villers-Bretonneux. The ticket-seller tried to discourage them from travelling further, but they hadn't crossed the world to be turned back so close to their goal. Tiney was glad to have Martin Woolf's letter detailing exactly what to say and do and who might help them when they reached the Somme. He had sent her five pages of advice, including two of intricate maps.

The railway lines across the north of France had been repaired since the Armistice, but outside the carriage windows, they saw the fields were ravaged. Even though this was the second spring since the war had ended, the fields were wastelands pockmarked by pools of stagnant water. Flowers and grass struggled to take hold in the poisoned ground. Miles and miles of rusty barbed wire had been rolled into huge mounds, as if all the land could yield was the ugly fruit of conflict. Scars of war lay in every direction; blackened stumps and trees stripped of all foliage pointing skywards like accusing fingers.

At Villers-Bretonneux, they were the only passengers to disembark. There was no one to meet them at the station, though Martin had said he would send a note to friends who lived there. As they gathered up their baggage, the sound of an explosion made Mrs Alston jump in alarm. She put her hand to her chest.

'What do you think that was?' she asked.

'Don't worry, Mummy, the war really is over,' said Ida. She hooked her arm through her mother's and set about finding a path through the rubble of the old railway station.

They walked through the town in silence. It was as if the war had only ended the day before they'd arrived. Villers-Bretonneux was like a vision of the world after the Apocalypse. No house remained completely intact. The old church was a shell with one wall remaining. Nearly every roof of every building had been blown away. They could see straight inside some of the ruins, and there was nothing left of most of the houses but dust and rubble. Tiney had read that the citizens had returned last July, but if so, few of them were about. Three little boys in ragged clothes wearing French soldiers' caps stood silently watching them from atop a pile of rubble.

Up ahead they saw a large tent with the sign of the Red Cross outside. A tall, broad-shouldered woman with dark hair cropped short was standing outside the tent opening, talking to a group of soldiers. She was dressed in a greatcoat, but beneath it she wore a white nurse's apron. When she saw the three strangers approaching she strode over to meet them. The woman's eyes were like pale beacons in her face and her mouth was drawn down with tiredness but Tiney could see that under other circumstances she could have been described as beautiful.

'Miss Flynn, Miss and Mrs Alston? I'm Ettie Rout. Martin Woolf wrote that I might expect you,' she said, kissing each of them on both cheeks, as a Frenchwoman might in greeting. 'Rather busy here this morning. An unexploded shell caught one of the Chinese labourers. Luckily, only a nick this time. I've just finished bandaging him. You must make sure you keep to the roads and well-trodden paths around Villers-Bretonneux. You can't know whether the ground is safe. There are unexploded munitions everywhere. The spring wildflowers can cover the most deceptive ground.'

Mrs Alston looked confused for a moment, then stepped back and fiddled with the clasp of her handbag. 'Can you please direct us to the Imperial Graves Commission?' she said stiffly. 'We have directions to my son's grave – Sheet 32 C J. 27. C. 32,' Mrs Alston recited as she took a neatly folded letter from her handbag and stared down at the details. 'But we can't decipher exactly what that means.'

'Mother,' said Ida, 'Nurse Rout isn't a tour guide. She's in charge of the Red Cross depot.'

'Call me Ettie, please,' said Nurse Rout. 'The Imperial Graves Commission has set up at the Red Chateau outside town and they might be able to help you. But I'm afraid there's no accommodation here. Best to take the evening train back to Amiens.' She looked at Mrs Alston with a particularly dubious expression.

'A friend suggested it might be possible to pay for a billet with a local family,' said Ida. 'We're happy to pitch in. We're used to hard work. Tiney and I worked in the kitchens of the Cheer-Up Hut in Adelaide, and Mother's a trouper. We could make ourselves useful cheering up the volunteers with the Australian Graves Detachment.'

Ettie Rout sighed, obviously not impressed. 'I don't think that would be possible. There aren't many buildings with roofs on them yet – most families have only one or two usable rooms. They're still using tarpaulins to cover the broken roofs and oiled paper in place of windows, and they burn bits of the house to keep themselves warm. However, if you're game, I could offer you camp beds for the night in the cellar of the school. There's little to eat here but if you'll give us a hand with serving lunch to the children you're welcome to join us.'

Inside the ruins of the old schoolhouse, dozens of raggedy children gathered around a long table. The room echoed with their shouts and the noisy clatter of spoons hitting against tin bowls. Mrs Alston was shown where the camp beds in the cellar were, while Ida and Tiney took off their coats and rolled up their sleeves. A soldier carrying two buckets of water from the town pump emptied them into metal tubs. Tiney and Ida set to work washing tin mugs, plates and spoons to serve the next round of children that arrived to be fed.

A small, dark-eyed boy came and stood beside Tiney, watching her with curiosity. She asked him in her schoolgirl French if he wanted something.

'I would like some black coffee and a cigarette,' he replied, in broken English.

Tiney laughed at first but when she looked into his face, she realised he was serious. Then she noticed he was using a crutch to support himself. The lower half of his left leg was missing.

When the children's lunch was finished, Ettie invited Tiney, Ida and Mrs Alston to join the workers for a bowl of stew and a cup of tea. The stew appeared to be mostly made of tinned vegetables and the tea was both weak and oddly bitter but the bread that was served with it was still warm from the oven.

Ettie introduced them to her fiancé, a man called Fred Hornibrook, and a young Frenchwoman who was apparently the teacher of the raggedy children. As they ate, a ragbag assortment of soldiers in various uniforms came in and out of the building.

Mrs Alston stiffened when a group of German soldiers appeared in the doorway and then left again. Moments later, several Chinese men arrived carrying supplies that they piled up in a corner at Ettie's direction.

'There are about four thousand German prisoners and a Chinese labour battalion in the area,' explained Ettie. 'They're working on the clean-up. The Chinese did most of the work rebuilding the railway line. The Australians here are volunteers who've chosen to stay behind and work with the Graves Detachments. They wanted to make sure that Australian soldiers buried their own rather than leave it to the British. But there are English and French soldiers too, still waiting to be called home – forgotten contingents. They keep body and soul together by selling army supplies to the villagers.'

'And the Graves Commission is working out of this place called the Red Chateau?' asked Ida.

'They're not very excited about civilians coming to the Front,' said Fred Hornibrook.

'Even if they aren't welcoming, we have to ask,' said Tiney. 'We think Charlie may be in the Adelaide Cemetery.'

'I'd take you there but I've injured my shoulder, worse luck.

Let's go outside and see if there's a vehicle available or a man who could take you out in my little trap.'

In the ruins of the town square, they saw a line of elderly women struggling under the weight of buckets of water taken from the town pump. Tiney helped one silver-haired old woman and Ida another, while Fred tried to organise transport for them.

Suddenly, a motorbike came roaring around the corner and pulled up outside the depot, sending a spray of mud into the air. When the rider pulled off his leather cap and goggles, Tiney knew him instantly.

'Martin Woolf, well, I'll be blowed!' called Fred Hornibrook, striding across the road to shake his hand and clap him on the shoulder.

'Isn't that your big bad wolf from Beachy Head?' asked Ida.

'Don't, Ida,' said Tiney. It was the strangest feeling to see Martin in this place, as if they were meeting again on another planet rather than in another country.

'Hello again,' said Martin, smiling directly at Tiney.

'Hello,' she replied, annoyed that her voice sounded squeaky and childish. 'I wanted to write a note to thank you for your letter but you didn't provide a return address.'

'I was about to leave England for some months,' he said. 'I could have given you an address in Paris or Geneva but I thought that would require a rather long explanation.'

At that moment, Ettie came outside. When she saw Martin she let out a shout of pleasure and ran over to embrace him. Tiney looked at the ground and felt strangely deflated as Ettie and Martin chatted like old friends.

'I wonder if you could hitch up Fred's trap and take these ladies out to the Red Chateau,' said Ettie.

'For you, anything,' he said. Ettie laughed.

Tiney set her lips firm, determined not to mind how they spoke to each other. 'I'm sure if you could just take us to the Adelaide Cemetery, we'd be able to find Charlie's grave ourselves,' she said.

'If you have a letter from the Imperial Graves commission, I could spare you the unhappiness of a long search,' said Martin. 'I know the Adelaide Cemetery well.'

He was looking at Ida and Mrs Alston as he spoke and Tiney felt moved by his compassion for them.

In the end, Martin and Fred went to collect the trap together. A truck drove past and a terrible odour caught Tiney unawares, making her feel a little dizzy. It was of earth and mud and mould and something else she couldn't quite identify. She saw Ettie's gaze flick towards the truck and away again.

'I should warn you,' said Ettie, 'the reason they try to ban civilians from visiting the battlefields is that you might experience something very disturbing. I was surprised Martin sent you to me. Last year, when he was working here with the Graves Detachment, an Englishwoman went into shock when she came across the remains of her son. They've exhumed thousands of bodies and they're trying to identify them, but it's going to take years to set things in order. You must brace yourselves for some difficult sights. You're very lucky that your young man is in a marked grave.' Then she shook their hands and went back into the Red Cross tent. As soon as she was out of sight, Mrs Alston grabbed Ida by the arm.

'Do you realise who that terrible woman really is?' whispered Mrs Alston, her voice catching as she spoke, as if she might choke. 'The Archbishop of Canterbury described her as the wickedest woman in the whole of the British Empire!'

'She doesn't seem either terrible or wicked to me,' said Ida. 'She seems quite kind, even if she isn't very elegant.'

'She must be awfully brave to stay in this place,' said Tiney, trying to steer the conversation into calmer waters. 'It's as if the war isn't over.'

As if to confirm Tiney's statement, another explosion from a distant field made the three women jump.

Recovering from her shock, Mrs Alston drew herself up to her full height. 'That's all well and good, but that woman, who is living in sin with that Hornibrook chap, is the same person who stood on the railway platforms of Paris handing out prophylactics to the soldiers. And she gave them cards of "recommended" houses of shame to visit.'

'Well, bully for her,' said Ida. 'I think I recall reading about her now. She was trying to stop them coming home with dreadful diseases. I should have thanked her for sparing me and all my friends an awful fate.'

Tiney smiled, reminded of why she liked Ida so much. Ida and Mrs Alston glared at each other. Then Tiney stepped forward and laid a hand on each of their arms.

'We're here for Charlie,' she said. 'Let's find him.'

Just then, Martin drove a tired old mule and trap around the corner of a ruined building. The trap was a two-wheeled gig with a single long seat at the front and a small dicky seat at the back. Martin helped Mrs Alston and Ida onto the bench seat and then looked at Tiney apologetically. 'I'm sorry, Miss Flynn,' he said, frowning.

Tiney smiled. 'I'll be perfectly happy riding backwards.'

He lifted Tiney up and placed her on the seat as if she were a small child, but then he looked into her eyes and smiled and she felt a shiver of certainty that he saw her as a woman.

As they bumped along the pot-holed road, Tiney's stomach grew hollow. Across the fields lay the skeletal haystacks of barbed wire and deep gullies of mud. A few tufts of green sprang out of the dull ground but there were thousands of wooden crosses stretching in every direction as far as the eye could see.

When they reached the entrance of Adelaide Cemetery, Martin helped them down from the trap and led them through the gates. Though Ida and Mrs Alston had chatted to Martin on the drive out, they fell silent now. Martin took Mrs Alston's note from the Imperial Graves Commission with the information about where Charlie was buried.

'Stay on the paths,' he warned.

'Miss Rout has already told us about the danger,' said Ida, sounding surprisingly meek.

'It's not only the bombs you have to be careful of,' said Martin. 'There's broken ground you might stumble on, and things that don't bear thinking of beneath this earth.'

They passed through the gates of Adelaide Cemetery; the graves stretched out silently before them, thousands of small, white crosses contained in a few acres of ground. Every now and then there was a distant explosion, as if the echoes of war would never let the bodies rest.

Tiney took out her Kodak Brownie camera, Minna and Frank's farewell gift. Staring down through the viewfinder made her feel steadier. A distant line of ragged trees starting to bud in a lopsided way seemed the only living thing for miles. Flat, stricken fields stretched on either side of the cemetery. Tiney didn't want to include this surrounding desolation. She adjusted the focus of the camera onto a single grave and pressed the shutter.

Most of the graves had tiny, flimsy wooden crosses on them but some had larger ones, placed by comrades or family members who had been among the early pilgrims to the cemetery. Ahead of her, Ida, Mrs Alston and Martin Woolf had come to a stop.

The cross on Charlie's grave was dwarfed by the size of the two larger ones on graves either side. There was barely twelve inches between the placement of one marker and the next, and when Mrs Alston fell to her knees she was obliged to kneel on the other soldier's grave. Ida knelt down beside her and put her arm around her mother. Tiney raised her camera to take a picture but then lowered it quickly. It was too intimate, too personal. Tears spilled from her eyes.

'Let's give the Alstons a little time,' said Martin and he gently steered her between the lines of graves.

Further along the path, an old woman was slowly walking between the white crosses, peering at each one. A spray of violets lodged in the black band of her hat quivered as she wove her way through the cemetery. As Tiney and Martin drew closer they saw the woman was clutching a wreath and that she was trembling.

'I won't be a moment,' said Tiney, turning away from Martin.

'I don't know where to lay his flowers,' said the old woman, glancing up as Tiney approached.

'Do you have a letter with directions? Perhaps we can help you find him if you tell us the number of his grave.'

'But no one knows where my Walter rests, dear,' said the woman. 'They never found him. My Walter could be under any one of these crosses. You see, he's in an unmarked grave.

A mother should be able to sense where her boy is resting, shouldn't she? But I don't know which to choose. I only have to choose one, one that says that an unknown soldier lies resting there, and that may be my Walter's grave.'

The old woman looked into Tiney's eyes, pleading. Tiney thought for a moment and then said, 'Perhaps we could choose one together.' She took the woman's frail hand in her own and led her back to the grave that Tiney had first photographed. Martin walked behind them and the sense of his presence made Tiney feel strangely braver.

Tiney picked a small spray of wildflowers and together she and the old lady knelt down, side by side, and laid flowers on the grave of an unknown soldier.

23

Fractured

On the drive back to Villers-Bretonneux, they passed a detachment of soldiers loading hessian sacks into the back of a truck. Tiney understood what this meant, but she still found it almost impossible to believe that the contents of those limp sacks had once been living, breathing men.

'Don't look too closely, Miss Flynn,' said Martin, as if he sensed Tiney's thoughts, though his eyes were on the road ahead.

Martin glanced across at Mrs Alston, his brow furrowed. She hadn't spoken a word since they'd left the cemetery, and her eyes were glassy. Her fingers were entwined with Ida's and they both stared ahead at the dusty road back to the town.

That evening, after a simple meal of canned food, Mrs Alston quietly gave Ettie Rout a roll of francs.

'For the children,' she said.

Ida helped her mother downstairs into the cellar of the schoolhouse. A single candle on a wooden box lit the space. Ida lay down beside her mother on one of the narrow camp beds and they held each other silently.

Tiney could hear the subdued tones of Ettie Rout upstairs, and the soft rumble of men's voices. Leaving the Alstons to their grief, she climbed the stairs. Ettie, Fred and Martin were sitting with some soldiers, drinking from tin cups. Tiney sat on a stool beside Ettie and gratefully accepted a mug of black tea. One of the soldiers sitting next to Fred was trembling, his hands shaking as he raised a tin mug to his lips. The room felt close with the scent of men and whisky. Tiney took her cup and went to stand by an open doorway. Outside, in the town square, the shouts of drunken soldiers reverberated against the ruins of the buildings.

Martin came and stood behind her. 'Some of these men are traumatised by the work. In the evenings, drink is their only escape. You can't judge them for it.'

'I wasn't judging anyone,' said Tiney.

Martin shrugged. 'Many would.'

'If you knew me better, you'd know I'm not like that.'

'I'd like to know you better,' he said.

Tiney shifted uncomfortably from one foot to the other.

'But I didn't come to Villers-Bretonneux expecting to find you here,' said Martin, 'if that's what you're thinking.'

'You're not a very good mind-reader after all,' said Tiney, though he had read her hopes so clearly that she squirmed.

'I'm en route to Paris,' said Martin. 'I detoured here to see Ettie and Fred. They're going to London next month, and I wanted to see them before they left.'

'How do you know them?'

'I was with the Australian Graves Detachment last year for a few months. It's a labour of love but soul-destroying too. The volunteers try to work out who the men were, from tattoos or from markings if their uniforms are rotted away.'

'It doesn't bear thinking of,' said Tiney.

'It's ugly work but we want to do the right thing by our mates.

It makes me sick at heart we'll never know who all of them were. On my last week of service, I found two men from the Eleventh Field Ambulance, men that I'd worked alongside. It was a relief to know that they, at least, would rest in marked graves.'

A drunken soldier came stumbling through the darkness towards the canteen. Tiney moved away to let him through the door but he fell in a heap beside the entrance and sat with his head in his hands. Martin stepped outside and squatted down beside the man, offering him his mug of tea. Tiney slunk back to the fire and sat quietly to one side.

After Martin had guided the drunken soldier into a corner of the room to escape the cold night, he came and joined Tiney by the fireside.

'Is he all right?' asked Tiney.

Martin shrugged. 'Some of these men have simply been forgotten. There are British soldiers left behind in charge of dumps of cars and ammunitions that have been completely abandoned by the army. The soldiers sell off what they can to the peasants in exchange for food and then spend the rest on drink.'

'Were you driven to drink when you worked here?'

'I was driven to the edge of despair.'

'Then why have you come back to France?' asked Tiney. 'Why don't you go home?'

'I've been working with the League of Nations Union in London. I'm on assignment for them now. Keeping the peace is a far greater challenge than winning the war.'

'But your family must be longing to see you,' said Tiney. 'They must be so proud of you.'

Martin didn't meet her gaze. He stared into the fire and the light flickered in his dark eyes. 'You know they called it "The

War for Civilisation", but it turned men into beasts. How can anyone be proud of that?'

'I'm proud of my brother,' said Tiney. 'And of Charlie Alston and all the men who died for us.'

'You aren't responsible for your brother's death, Tiney.'

Tiney recoiled. 'That's not what I meant. But he fought to protect me, to protect Australia.'

'Do you really think that was what the war was about? You told me, when we stood on the cliffs of Beachy Head, that you weren't naive.'

Tiney was suddenly so unspeakably angry that she couldn't reply. She stood up abruptly, dropping her tin mug on the stone floor. Everyone turned in surprise at the clattering sound.

'Goodnight,' she said, trying to keep her voice steady. She didn't look back at Martin. She crept down the stairs to lie in her narrow camp bed in the dark, listening to the mournful weeping of Ida and Mrs Alston.

The next day, feeling dusty and exhausted, they climbed back onto the eastbound train, away from the Somme. Although they had planned to travel on to Albert in search of Louis' grave, Mrs Alston was so patently unwell Ida had said they had no choice but to return to Amiens and find a decent hotel to allow her to recover.

Tiney nodded. It was as if the silence of the cemeteries had entered her throat and she couldn't find words to express any of her thoughts or feelings.

When Martin emerged and offered to help carry their bags, she responded curtly, 'We can manage.'

'I'm not worried about you,' he said, as he picked up the Alstons' suitcases. 'But I am worried about Mrs Alston and Ida.

Sometimes, the thing we pray for is the thing that undoes us.'

'I won't let the thing I pray for undo me,' said Tiney as they picked their way through the rubble at the entrance of the railway station.

'The unbreakable Miss Flynn,' said Martin. 'But you should be careful of fractures. Grief can be shattering.'

'That's neither helpful nor encouraging,' said Tiney.

'Would you prefer I said something glib and untrue?'

Tiney blushed. 'No, of course I wouldn't.'

They stood in awkward silence on the platform until the train arrived. Martin handed their baggage onto the train and saw Mrs Alston and Ida to their seats. As he exited the carriage, he brushed past Tiney, who was standing in the breezeway, having dealt with the porter and the ticket inspector.

'I'm sorry, Tiney. I was too brusque last night. I think it's truly courageous of you to be making this pilgrimage and honouring your brother. I wish I had better connections in Albert or Tincourt that could help you.'

Tiney softened. 'You've been very helpful already. I never would have been able to work out where the Buire British Cemetery was if you hadn't sent me your map, and I'm sure I'll find a driver in Albert at the place you suggested.'

'Will you write to me? Tell me how you fare?'

He scribbled an address in Paris onto a slip of paper and gave it to her as she stood on the steps of the train. Tiney folded the note and put it carefully into her bag. When she looked up, Martin was already walking away but though she didn't call his name, he suddenly turned to wave, as if he sensed she was watching him, as if he could read her mind.

As soon as they reached Amiens they checked into the nearest hotel to the railway station and Ida put her mother to bed.

That evening, Ida and Tiney sat at a small table in a cafe while Mrs Alston slept.

'I'm sorry, Tiney,' said Ida. 'We will come with you to find Louis' grave, just as I promised, but I must give Mummy time to regain her strength. I've telephoned friends in Paris. I think we should take Mummy there for a week or two, get her settled in, then you and I can travel to Albert together.'

Tiney was silent for some time. Finally, she found her voice.

'I can go on alone,' she said.

'No, you can't,' said Ida. 'You're only eighteen years old and we promised your parents we'd chaperone you.'

'Ettie said there were women younger than me working as VADs during the war.'

'That was different, Tiney,' said Ida. 'I'm sure she wasn't expecting you to head off on your own. The war may be over but the peace is hardly won.'

'That's more or less what Martin said. But he was encouraging. And he has given me very good directions. It's not as though I'll be wandering about like a lost lamb. I know exactly where to find Louis' grave.'

'That Martin Woolf – he could very well be a wolf in sheep's clothing for all we know. You should be careful. What do we know about him? Don't you think it a little too much of a coincidence that he wrote to you, with no return address, and then turned up at Villers-Bretonneux?'

'If only it was because of me! But he was there to see Ettie

Rout, not me. He didn't know our visits would coincide. He's on his way to Paris to work for the League of Nations Union.'

'Is he Jewish? With a name like Woolf, you can't help but wonder.'

'Stop it, Ida. Martin has nothing to do with my wanting to go on alone. When I saw you and your mother at Charlie's graveside I understood that you both needed time, just the two of you, without me. And that I need to find Louis' grave on my own.'

Suddenly, Ida began to weep. 'You won't feel so bold once you've seen it. Oh Tiney, I thought it would make me feel stronger, that being able to see where he lay would heal something in me, but it only made me realise that I'm broken inside. When I saw that sad little grave, when I saw where he is, the place that he fought and died, it was as if it shone a light on a great black chasm, a horrible echo chamber that's inside my heart, the place where all my love for my Charlie used to be. I feel so empty.'

Tiney wrapped her arms around Ida. She stroked her hair away from her face and kissed her. She didn't care that the waiters might see. She knew that all across France, women were weeping for their lost brothers, sons and lovers.

'You go to Paris, Ida,' she said, softly. 'I'll come to you soon. Then we'll walk along the Seine together and see Paris in the spring. But for now, you have to let me go.'

The next day, Tiney waved Ida and Mrs Alston off from Amiens station as they set out for Paris. Then she crossed to the opposite platform and sat with her small cardboard suitcase waiting for the train to Arras. She would need to travel deep into the Somme to reach the ruined town of Albert. She took Martin's map from her handbag and smoothed it out on her lap.

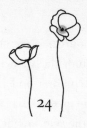

Beneath the everlasting sky

A swirl of dust swept into Tiney's face as she alighted from the train in the late morning. The spring sunshine was bright and warm but, like Villers-Bretonneux, the town of Albert was a landscape of ruins. Tiney remembered Louis sending a postcard from Albert of the 'Leaning Mary', a statue of the Virgin which had teetered on the ruined tower of the basilica, but was now lost in the wreckage of the town.

Clutching her suitcase, Tiney made her way along a dusty path through a construction site where a dozen men were clearing away debris. From the other side of the station she could see a jumbled assortment of half-built and half-destroyed buildings. Not far away there was a line of old cars parked outside what looked like a hotel, and further down the street was a newly built red-brick building.

Tiney tramped down to the hotel and negotiated with a burly Frenchman to hire a car to take her to Buire-Courcelles. She drew out Martin's map and pointed to where the Buire British Cemetery was located, and the Frenchman whistled to a younger man and waved him over to study the map; then they insisted she pay in advance.

The drive to Buire-Courcelles seemed to take forever. Once again, Tiney felt as though the silence of the battlefields had stolen her voice, and she couldn't find any words to speak to the driver of the car. She sat in the back seat, her suitcase on her lap, staring fiercely out the window at the patchwork of fields and hedgerows. A few small boys waved and shouted as they sped past. The car lurched to avoid a farm-cart and then turned into open green fields, a landscape untouched by mortar fire and trenches. In the villages outside of Albert, there was not a sign of khaki and no flags flew, but a few German prisoners were pulling down some military huts under the supervision of a bored-looking gendarme.

Tiney's whole body trembled as the car drew closer to the tiny hamlet of Buire-Courcelles. Her heart hammered in her chest and her ribs ached. The old car crossed a bridge and drove past a line of simple brick and stone houses, and then the driver turned right along a narrow laneway and pulled up outside a small cemetery. A few young trees grew along its boundary but beyond were fields of green spring grass.

Tiney climbed out of the car, uncertain whether she should ask the driver to wait. She glanced at the quiet countryside about her. A few starlings flew out of the eaves of a nearby house. It was as if the war hadn't reached this tiny corner of the Somme. It gave her the confidence to ask the driver if he could return for her late in the afternoon.

At the entrance to the cemetery, Tiney hesitated. She put her suitcase down beside the gate. This was the moment she had dreamt of for more than a year. She could still see herself, sitting on the steps of Larksrest, opening Louis' last letter. She wanted to call out his name, as if to let him know she had finally reached him. Then she shut her eyes and tried to imagine each one of her sisters standing beside her along with Mama and Papa – all six of them walking through the gateway together. The gravel crunched beneath her feet as she stepped into the cemetery, her eyes shut tight.

When she opened them again, the cemetery seemed almost disappointingly small, so different to the vast Adelaide Cemetery of Villers-Bretonneux. The same white crosses marked the military graves, but there were civilian graves here as well. A small, weathered stone crypt stood to the right of the entry to the cemetery.

Tiney trod carefully, as if for fear of waking the dead. She stopped before each white cross and read the inscriptions, the names of each of the fallen. And then she found Louis.

He lay in a row of Australian soldiers who had died within days of each other. Tiney stood, very still, very quiet, before his cross and stared. She couldn't make tears come, though an ocean of longing swelled inside her.

'Hello, Louis,' she said, kneeling down at the edge of his grave and resting her hand on the earth that covered her brother.

Once she had spoken his name, it was as if a spell had broken. Words began to flow from her mouth, tales of everything that had happened since that long-ago day in 1914 when Louis last walked down the path of Larksrest, under the lychgate and out into the street for the very last time. She told the story of each of their sisters, as if Louis was sitting right in front of her, resting against the wooden cross, laughing and smoking a cigarette. She imagined him furrowing his brow with concern when she talked of Papa's illness, and smiling at the news of the birth of little Ray Junior. She talked until every detail of the past year had been recounted, the long terrible months since his death, right up to her last conversation with Martin Woolf.

When all the stories were told, Tiney opened her handbag and took out three sprigs of wattle. Each of her sisters had picked a spray of wattle to place on Louis' grave, and though the soft yellow blossom had grown dry and faded in its journey across the world, the small buds of gold looked bright against the base of the white cross. Then carefully, tenderly, she pulled out the weeds that grew in clumps on the grave. With her fingers, she scraped a place for a bouquet of wildflowers that she gathered from around the edge of the cemetery. Over by the stone crypt, sheltered from the wind, was a cluster of early poppies. Tiney picked six of the blood-red flowers, one for each of the Flynns, and laid them in a crisscross pattern on top of Louis' grave. Then she picked three more poppy flowers and tucked them carefully into the folds of a handkerchief. Finally, satisfied she had done all she could, she dusted her hands and knees and stood at the foot of the grave again.

'Louis,' she said. 'Louis.'

Her eyes began to stream, tears washing down her face. Not wanting to dampen her handkerchief of poppies, she wiped the tears away with the back of her hand but didn't sob or make any sound. Inside her was a stillness so deep, so profound it was as if she had been hollowed out. She felt like a bell, as if the touch of another human being might set her ringing, a sound so pure and sad that everyone would weep when they heard it.

When Tiney walked through the gate of the cemetery, it was as if she had crossed over from another world. The quiet lane, the dappled afternoon light that shone through the trees, the soft twittering of birds – all were foreign and disorienting. From very far away, she heard an explosion as if from another universe. She wished she'd asked the driver to wait. She sat on her suitcase, feeling dazed, and watched the sun sink behind the trees. But still the car didn't return.

When the sky had taken on an evening glow, an old woman in a white bonnet came slowly up the laneway. She wore a faded blue skirt and black bodice. She stopped on the verge beside the cemetery, close to Tiney, and then bent over painfully to cut a handful of grass. Tiney guessed she was at least eighty years old and tried to to imagine all the things her eyes had seen in a lifetime. She would have been a young girl in 1848 when Tiney's great-grandparents fled the uprisings in Europe and sailed to South Australia. Now the old woman had borne witness to 'the war to end all wars'. Perhaps she had even seen soldiers carrying Louis' body into the cemetery.

The old lady looked up and nodded at Tiney. Her dark eyes shone in her brown, lined face. She held out a fistful of the cut grass and said, '*Pour mes lapins.*'

Tiney understood she was simply gathering grass for her rabbits. Before Tiney could think of a reply, the old lady began to walk away but then turned and limped back. She took Tiney by the hand.

'*Venez avec moi, ma fille,*' she said.

Tiney allowed herself to be led down the lane to a cluster of huts. The old lady introduced herself as Madame Sentier and settled Tiney on a bench outside the hut in the last of the sun's rays. She chatted to Tiney in French as she opened a small pen and laid the cut grass before two large brown rabbits. Night fell yet still the driver hadn't returned. Madame Sentier came outside and led Tiney into her hut to show her that she had made up an extra bed.

They ate supper together in silence – vegetable soup, stewed dried apples spread on chunks of bread, fresh egg, tea and goat's milk. That night, Tiney slept as though she were a little girl again, as though the war had never happened, as though she was born to live in the country, to live quietly with the old French grandmother.

It took three days for Tiney, with Madame Sentier's help, to arrange another car to take her back to Albert so she could return to Amiens and from there to Paris. She was glad of the quiet days with the old French woman. Madame Sentier's pleasure in her company was obvious, even though Tiney's schoolgirl French didn't lend itself to long conversations. In the evenings, they sat together by the small fire and Madame Sentier told Tiney of her family, all lost in the war, of her home in a small village on the Belgian border that was razed to the ground and of her years of wandering in search of a safe place to rest. And of how she had found peace in the tiny hut that was built for the refugees fleeing the conflicts. On the morning of Tiney's fourth day in Buire-Courcelles, she bade Madame Sentier goodbye.

'*Bon courage,*' said the old woman, as she held Tiney's hands.

'You have been so kind. One day, I hope to come back to see you again,' said Tiney. '*Merci beaucoup pour votre gentillesse. Je ne vous oublierai jamais, Madame Sentier.*'

Madame Sentier smiled through tears. 'But it is not goodbye,' she said in French. 'It is farewell. You will never visit me again. I will die far from my home, for my village is no more. But you will go and make a new world, you and all the other young ones. You must do this, little one. Remake the world.'

Artist's model

Ida's studio was reached by climbing a twisting stone staircase in an old apartment building in the Latin Quarter. The stairwell smelt of damp but Ida's room was bright with sunlight streaming through a dormer window that overlooked the boulevard below. There was very little furniture – a narrow single bed, a table, two chairs, her easel and a clutter of art materials arranged on a bookshelf. A small, gold-framed, oval portrait of Charlie hung beside the bed, and Ida's sketches, watercolours and small canvases were tacked up to cover the fading wallpaper.

They sat in a patch of sunlight near the window. Ida had bought crisp bread rolls in anticipation of Tiney's arrival, and set a jug of chocolate and another of black coffee on the table. Then she carried two small dishes, one with pale yellow butter, the other with *confiture*, from the makeshift kitchen wedged into a corner of the room.

'You must stay with me as long as you like,' said Ida. She put her hand on Tiney's knee and smiled. 'I never should have let you go to Buire-Courcelles without me. If I'd known you'd take so long before joining us, I would have dragged you to Paris kicking and screaming and made you wait until I could come with you. If anything had happened to you, your parents would never have forgiven me. Why on earth did you stay on in Amiens for a week on your own?'

'I needed to simply sit and write letters,' said Tiney. 'Each letter to my sisters took me a whole day to write and then it took another whole day to write to my parents. I wanted to finish all the letters and then send them together so no one could feel left out. And I had to write to my uncle and aunt as well.'

Tiney couldn't tell Ida that she'd also written to Martin every day she was in Amiens. In her mind's eye, that week would forever conjure a vision of the small corner cafe with red check tablecloths where she would sit each day, with her letter-writing folio, a bottle of ink and her fountain pen. She could see her hand moving across the paper, words pouring out of her, and a *cafe au lait* that she nursed all day until it was cold, as she wrote minute descriptions of the days in Buire-Courcelles and all it had meant to her. As if a letter a day wasn't enough, she'd written to Martin twice on the day before she left Amiens for Paris.

'You could have written your letters from here,' said Ida. 'By the way, Mummy and I collected all our mail from the Thomas Cook agency. There were some for you too.' She jumped up and fetched a pile of envelopes from her bedside table. There were six for Tiney, one from each of her sisters, one each from Mama and Papa and one from Onkel Ludwig and Tante Bea. Tiney shuffled through them twice, unable to stop the twinge of disappointment that there wasn't one from Martin.

'Don't open them now,' said Ida. 'I don't want to lose you to homesickness. If Thea's letters make *me* homesick I can't imagine what it will do to you. We have to savour being here, Tiney. Every minute of it. Paris is beautiful at the moment.'

'It was so lovely to arrive here, to be somewhere that isn't spoiled by war,' said Tiney. 'It's hard to imagine what it must be like to live with all that desolation day in and day out.'

'You need time to recover. Lord knows, Mummy and I were shattered after Villers-Bretonneux. Mummy didn't want to stay in Paris more than a week before going back to Sussex to be with Mrs Bloomfield. The only good thing about you taking so long to join us was that it helped my case of convincing Mummy that I simply had to stay on here.'

Ida leaned forward, her eyes bright. 'You have no idea, Tiney, the number of Australian women painters I've met since I arrived. Evelyn Chapman is here – she was the first artist to paint Villers-Bretonneux in 1918. And Agnes Goodsir, a simply astonishing painter from Portland, is here – and so many American and British painters and writers. You can be a woman painter in Paris, make real art, and not be treated like a childish amateur. And Paris is so cheap, too. You could live here for a whole year on the smell of an oily rag.'

'It sounds wonderful, Ida. I wish I could stay.'

'You must stay, Tiney. We'll have such fun.'

'I've been thinking I might make a short trip, maybe to Berlin or Heidelberg. You know Mama's family were German. I think it would mean a lot to Mama and to my Onkel and Tante. They did pay my fare.'

'Germany! Are you mad? Didn't you read about the Kapp Putsch?'

'I couldn't get English newspapers in Amiens,' said Tiney. 'And I was too busy writing letters to struggle with the French ones.'

'A whole brigade of German soldiers took Berlin earlier in the month. The workers went out on strike and so the nasty little uprising failed, but as the soldiers left the city they opened fire on the crowds. The putsch may have failed but there's nothing to say there won't be another. And there are terrible things happening in the Ruhr. They shot twelve Red Cross nurses! Germany simply isn't safe. You mustn't even dream of going, Tiney.'

Tiney stood up and went to the window and looked out over the rooftops of Paris. 'I may never come to Europe again. I can't fritter away my time and money here in Paris. And there are other things too...things I need to do.'

'You have to take some time for yourself, Tiney. Visit the galleries, sit in a cafe and write more letters home. You could even come to the life drawing classes with me.'

'Ida, I can't draw. You know that's your gift and Thea's, not mine.'

'You could come to our classes as a model. I'd love to draw you and to see how the other artists render you too.'

'You mean take my clothes off? In front of strangers?'

Ida laughed. 'You have a lovely face, Tiney. We need a portrait model at our life drawing class, as well as a life model. You could keep your clothes on. The artists all pitch in and pay the models. It wouldn't be much but it would cover your costs of staying in Paris until you've thought about what you want to do next.'

'You mean they'd pay me to sit for them?' said Tiney, suddenly feeling brighter.

'It's harder work than it sounds. You have to be very still and you can't let your expression flit about the way it's doing right this minute.'

Ida took Tiney's chin in her hand and turned her face towards the spring sunshine. 'Your face has changed. Your cheekbones seem higher, your features more etched. I can't wait to paint you.'

The worn floorboards of the atelier were flecked with paint and the space smelt of linseed oil and turpentine. Podiums were positioned at either end of the long room. A woman in a tattered kimono sat on the edge of the far podium, smoking a cigarette. She waved and blew a kiss as Ida entered the studio and Ida winked at her before leading Tiney over to the second podium. Tiney took off her coat and hat and sat meekly on a stool while Ida combed her hair.

'That's better,' said Ida. 'We must keep all that unruly gold fluff away from your face.'

'Is there anything I should do?' whispered Tiney.

'Simply sit, without twitching that cheeky mouth of yours. We'll work in twenty-minute sessions. And do try to keep your gaze steady.'

After ten minutes, Tiney developed an itch on her back and it took all her concentration to not flinch. She was aware of a man standing to her left, sketching her profile, just out of the line of her peripheral vision. When Ida finally called 'Time!' and Tiney was allowed to move again, she turned to look at the man. It was Martin Woolf. He was standing by the window, with light flooding in from behind him. When Tiney met his gaze, he smiled.

'Hello again,' he said.

Tiney climbed down from the podium and crossed over to look at the drawing that he had made of her. It was a simple charcoal sketch that looked nothing like her.

Martin laughed at her bemused expression. 'I know. I'm not much of an artist,' he confessed.

'Then why are you here?'

'The concierge at Ida's said I'd probably find you here.'

'That doesn't really answer my question,' said Tiney.

'I had to see you and thank you for your letters, your beautiful, shining, wonderful letters.'

Tiney looked down at her feet. When she'd written the letters, it was like writing them to a part of herself, almost without believing that Martin would actually read them.

Ida came over to them and interrupted. 'Tiney, we only take short breaks to begin with – could you please get back on the podium? We can have a cup of tea after the next round.'

Martin looked flustered. 'Sorry for holding you up. I won't stay,' he said. 'I don't think I can do your portrait justice but I would like to ask if you'd join me for dinner this evening.'

'Martin, darling, I'm not sure I approve,' said Ida teasingly. 'And how can you leave *me* out of your plans when I'm your favourite dance partner?'

'You'd be welcome to come along,' said Martin, deflated.

It was the prompt that Tiney needed. She looked Martin directly in the eyes and said, 'I would love to have dinner with you. I'm sure Ida is only teasing and far too busy to join us, aren't you, Ida?'

'Touché, Tiney Flynn,' said Ida. 'Paris is having the right effect on you.'

Tiney scribbled Ida's address onto a scrap of paper. 'I'll meet you in the courtyard of Ida's apartment at seven thirty. There's a seat outside the concierge's. I'll wait for you there.'

Ida laughed and took Tiney's arm, dragging her towards the podium.

'You certainly have changed, Tiney. If I didn't know better,

I'd say you're turning into quite the flapper.'

Later, as Tiney and Ida walked back to the apartment, Tiney asked, 'Where did you dance with Martin?'

'At a party last week. But he danced with half the women there. He seems to know everyone in the Australian circles in Paris – or everyone knows him. He rubs shoulders with the most provocative people – the socialists, the pacifists, the Americans, and he talks as if he has entree to every salon in Paris.' Ida turned and smiled at Tiney. 'A tall, dark, mysterious stranger will come into your life…'

'Stop it, Ida,' said Tiney, blushing.

'Tiney Flynn! That blush is very becoming. No wonder Martin is charmed. But it is Paris and it is spring, so don't you do anything I wouldn't do. Actually, I take that back. Don't do anything I *would* do – or at least anything that will get me into trouble with your sisters.'

That evening, Tiney almost had to pinch herself. She couldn't quite believe that she was walking along the banks of the Seine with a man on a warm spring evening. Martin offered her his arm as they climbed the steps. They crossed over from the Left Bank to the Right Bank across the Pont Royal and then walked past the Tuileries.

Martin had chosen a cafe on the Champs-Élysées. Tiney had never imagined a setting as beautiful. She had that strange sensation that she'd first had on the ship coming over that she was suspended between two worlds, as if she were living a life that belonged in a book, not the life of an ordinary young woman from Adelaide.

They talked of Martin's work with the League of Nations

Union, and his hopes of securing a position with the newly formed International Labour Organisation in Geneva. When he asked her to tell him more about her life, she laughed.

'You already know all about me and my family, yet you haven't told me anything about *your* family,' said Tiney.

'My mother lives in Victor Harbor still,' said Martin. 'She's a Quaker, a pacifist, the gentlest woman in the world. She wasn't happy about my signing up, even though I was a stretcher-bearer and didn't fire a gun.'

'And your father?' asked Tiney.

Martin cradled his glass and didn't look at Tiney for a long moment.

'My father was a German Jew. He left Germany because he objected to the Kaiser's militarism. He met my mother in England, where I was born, and then we emigrated to South Australia when I was a small boy. My father had become a naturalised Australian a few years before war broke out, but he was interned at Holdsworthy in 1915.'

'My cousin was at Holdsworthy too,' said Tiney.

Martin didn't meet her gaze. 'There were more than six thousand prisoners held at Holdsworthy. He was an older man, quiet. He kept to himself.'

'And is he home with your mother again?'

'No, he was extradited to Germany last September. But he never reached Europe. He died of a heart attack on board ship.'

Tiney reached across the table and took Martin's hand. He had seemed so strong, so sure of himself at Villers-Bretonneux she hadn't imagined he carried a burden of secret grief.

'I'm so sorry,' she said.

'I'm glad I can tell you. It's not the sort of thing that I'd share with many people.'

'I feel I can tell you things that I can't tell anyone else, too,' said Tiney. 'About my cousin Will and my family. I'm so grateful to you for helping me find Louis' grave. I think it made me understand much more about grief.'

'My father was buried at sea,' said Martin. 'I was thinking of him that first time we met, at Beachy Head. Whenever I look at the ocean, I can feel his presence.'

'It's strange, isn't it, how you can feel as though the spirit of someone you've lost is in a landscape? I can understand how the sea would make you feel that way. I feel closer to Louis just being in France, in the country where he died.'

Martin nodded.

'Martin,' said Tiney, suddenly nervous. 'I think I need to find my cousin Will's grave too, for my uncle and aunt's sake as much as my own. I wouldn't be here if they hadn't helped me.'

'There's a new group organised that plans to care for the German war graves. They're called *Deutsche Kreigsgraberfursorge*. It might be worth writing to them but you should also write to the Red Cross. They've done a good job of tracking the German dead. But if your cousin is buried in Germany, I wouldn't advise you look for his grave. The government isn't stable and it's not safe yet.'

'I've just had a letter from my uncle and aunt – about my other cousin, Paul. The one who was in Holdsworthy. He's in Germany, in Berlin. If it's possible, I'd like to visit him.'

'Tiney, I don't think this is a good idea. The British aren't exactly popular in Germany at the moment.'

'You sound like Ida. But I speak German and I'm not actually British. I'm Australian.'

'Twelve Red Cross nurses in the Ruhr were murdered this week. Some of them may have been Australian. Being a beautiful young woman won't exempt you from harm.'

Tiney opened her mouth to reply but was suddenly ashamed. Instead of feeling grief at the thought of the twelve murdered nurses, all she could think of was that Martin had told her she was beautiful.

They talked until after midnight, until the cafe emptied of customers and the waiters began up-ending chairs onto tables, signalling they were about to close up for the night. Martin flagged a cab to drive them back to Ida's apartment in the Latin Quarter. When they reached Ida's, Martin asked the driver to wait while he saw Tiney to the gates.

'I leave for Geneva at the end of the week,' he said, taking Tiney's hand. 'But I'd like us to keep in touch.'

'I'd like that too,' said Tiney, waiting for the moment he would draw her into his arms.

Then Martin frowned, leaned forward, and kissed her on the top of her head, as if she were a child. Tiney took a step back. After all the letters and the long evening of intimate conversation, she'd expected something different.

'Goodnight, Martin,' she said. 'I hope things go well for you in Geneva.'

The concierge opened the gate for her and motioned her inside. She glanced over her shoulder. Martin was standing at the open door of the cab, watching her. She raised one hand in farewell, slipped through the doorway and burst into tears.

26

Langemarck

A plump Englishman took Tiney's battered cardboard suitcase, and flung it into the back of his car. 'You think the job at the school might suit, Miss Flynn?' he asked.

'I don't think I'm the person you're looking for,' said Tiney. 'I came to Europe to visit my brother's grave in the Somme. I have a cousin who died here in Belgium too. I'm not a qualified teacher.'

'You look like an educated young lady to me.'

'I'm sorry if there's been a misunderstanding,' said Tiney. 'I wrote to see about being billeted with the schoolteacher, but I'm very happy that there's a room at the Hôtel de la Gare.'

'I don't suppose you'd think of staying on after you've found your cousin's resting place?' he persisted. 'My little ones, their mum has this idea that if I talk English to them and she speaks Flemish, they'll work out both languages. But the little buggers don't seem to be able to learn to read either language. Charlotte's coming up six now, our first little war baby, and I'm right worried about her.'

'Are there a lot of Englishmen working in Ypres?'

'My word! Less than half the locals have come back. There's

talk of turning the whole town into a war memorial; others want to rebuild, make the old town what it was. The Imperial War Graves Commission is based here too and we don't have enough men to tackle the job of building the cemeteries. The Chinese Labour Corps are working on the battlefield clearance but there's no end of work needs doing. Visitors are banned from the Salient but we can't stop those with money and connections. And to be honest, I think it's good to see a loyal young lady like yourself make a pilgrimage for our brave boys.'

The jolly Englishman chatted all the way from the station to the hotel, as they drove through ruined streets full of rubble and destruction. The hotel looked as though it had been hastily repaired. The building was not much more than a shell, missing sections of walls and roof, its empty windows framing patches of blue sky. Most of the street was in ruins and only a few buildings were still standing. In the distance, small huts used as temporary housing sat clumped on the bleak plain like ugly mushrooms.

Before opening the door, Tiney turned to the driver and took a deep breath. 'As I said, I've come to find my cousin's grave. I was wondering if I could employ you to drive me out there tomorrow? The Red Cross sent me his details. He's in Lange-marck Cemetery.' She took the letter from her bag and unfolded it. 'I have a map of how to reach it.'

'That can't be right. Langemarck is a German cemetery. The Huns are renting the land they're buried in but they shouldn't be allowed to stay.'

'My cousin fought with the Germans,' said Tiney. She tried to keep her voice steady but she sensed the driver freeze.

'You shouldn't have come to Ypres,' he said, finally, his tone heavy and flat. 'The German cemeteries are dangerous. They're in a terrible state. You'll never find your cousin's grave. There's more than a million dead Boche in the Salient plain.'

Tiney folded the map and letter and put them back in her bag. A heaviness settled on her limbs and she could hardly bring herself to open the car door.

Martin had warned her against coming to Ypres. He'd even written her a letter from Geneva trying to dissuade her. Ida had told her the idea was ludicrous, that it was more than enough to have simply found the information about where Will was buried. No one expected her to go and visit his grave. Onkel Ludwig and Tante Bea had expressly said it wasn't necessary. But Tiney was determined. While Ida was away on a painting expedition with friends, Tiney spoke with some of the painters who had been to Ypres and made her plans. By the time Ida returned to Paris, Tiney was on her way to Belgium.

The driver unloaded Tiney's suitcase from the car and placed it on the ground outside the Hôtel de la Gare. Then he turned to face Tiney. 'The war will never be over for the people of this town,' said the Englishman, 'nor for any of us who survived it. The war exists in people's imaginations and memories and it will live on forever and ever. You should go home to your own country and get on with things.'

'Peace lives in the imagination too,' said Tiney, and suddenly she found herself quoting Martin. 'We need to make a place for peace.'

The driver didn't respond. He slammed the door of his car and sped off down the dusty roadway.

That evening, Tiney walked down to Skindles, a small restaurant that served simple Flemish food. It was housed in a temporary building at the end of the road. Tiney sat by the restaurant's coal-burning stove and ordered a bowl of what she thought was rabbit stew. There were two other tables of battlefield visitors in the small room as well as several local workers, many of them speaking in English, but after the reaction of the driver, Tiney wasn't keen to strike up a conversation. The room smelt close, of beer and tobacco, of fried onions and coal smoke. She slunk back to the hotel.

That night, Tiney hardly slept. In the early-morning light, before anyone else in the hotel awoke, she packed her bag and slipped out into the ruins of Ypres. Most of the residents were living in small and flimsy temporary houses made of wood and corrugated iron on the edge of the town. It was eerie walking past the shadows of the crushed and broken Cloth Hall. The medieval town was like a ghost town. No one was up and few birds sang as she made her way along the road to Langemarck Cemetery.

The German graveyard lay seven miles from town, through flat fields of devastation. As the sun rose, the poppies in the fields glowed like scarlet flame against the spring grass. Tiney felt as though she was walking through a dream. Along the verge, more red poppies were in bloom, as well as yellow buttercups and white Queen Anne's lace. She passed along an avenue of ruined trees, tiny green leaves struggling to bud through the blackened, broken trunks. She crossed small bridges over creeks, hastily reconstructed, walked past craters and piles of rubble, shattered farmhouses with nothing but a single section of wall remaining, deep trenches where water pooled and lay stagnant, and thousands and thousands of graves. Some bore white crosses, others had scattered headstones. Everywhere she looked, there were graves.

The sun had well and truly risen by the time she reached

Langemarck, where thousands of simple, unpainted crosses stretched across the field. A low hedge and a tangle of barbed-wire fences surrounded the cemetery. The slope from the road to the edge of the cemetery was slippery with mud and though she walked up and down the road, she couldn't see a point of entry. Tiney knew that crossing any land without a marked path could be dangerous. She remembered the small boy at Villers-Bretonneux with one leg. Then she noticed an older woman dressed in black moving among the graves. She moved with purpose, cutting small briar roses from a hedge and placing them before the yellowing crosses. Tiney waved to her.

'How did you get in?' she called, first in English, then in German. The woman's face relaxed when she heard Tiney speak German.

'Up ahead, follow me, I'll show you where I found a way through the wire,' she said.

As they walked in tandem either side of the barbed wire, Tiney said, 'I'm searching for my cousin's grave. He's buried here.'

'My cousin is here too.'

The woman stopped at a small break in the hedge and then, wrapping her shawl around her hand, she pushed aside a large coil of barbed wire and gestured for Tiney to climb through.

'My cousin, my brothers and my son are all in Belgian soil,' said the woman, offering her hand to Tiney as she clambered up the verge. 'There are more than a million German men and boys in Flanders fields.'

They walked together through the graves, both glancing from side to side to scan the tin nameplates tacked to the base of the crosses.

'My cousin died in the first battle of Ypres in 1915,' said Tiney.

'My brother died in the Somme. I've already been there to find his grave.'

'My husband died in the Somme. I've come to Belgium to find my cousin and my brothers, but especially to find my boy, my only son. He went missing in action in 1915. He was only eighteen. But you know, all these years, since he died, I can never feel he's truly dead. Perhaps missing in action might mean he lost his memory and came to live among the people here. Sometimes, I dream that he is living in Belgium. Perhaps he has a Belgian wife and a little child.'

Tiney had seen enough of the battlefields now to know how easy it would be for a man to be listed as 'missing in action' but truly dead. She looked at the woman with such pity that the woman began to weep.

'I must believe in this dream.'

'Dreams are important,' said Tiney, touching the woman gently on her shoulder.

Tiney remembered too well that feeling, that numbing disbelief that someone you loved so much could simply have been snuffed out. She remembered those moments of wanting to believe Louis' death had been some sort of terrible joke, that at any moment a letter would arrive to say it was all a mistake, that he was alive and on his way home to Adelaide. And she thought again of the photo of the woman and child, the desperate longing to believe that they might have been connected to Louis.

The woman suddenly, unexpectedly, embraced Tiney. Tiney felt how frail she was beneath her widow's weeds. Then the woman kissed her swiftly on one cheek and turned and hurried away. Tiney was left alone, surrounded by the yellowing wooden crosses.

When she finally reached the section of the cemetery that the Red Cross had designated as being where Will was buried, she discovered it was actually a mass grave. The tin plate simply said that the grave contained twenty-five soldiers. Her heart sank. She couldn't take a picture of this for her uncle and aunt. Instead, she gathered up handfuls of wildflowers and covered the length of the grave. She worked with speed and purpose until the grave looked as decorated as Louis' had been. Then she took a photograph of the blanket of flowers with her Brownie camera. Lastly, she knelt down and removed a small pinch from an envelope of poppy seeds that she'd gathered in the cemetery in Buire-Courcelles and buried them near the grave marker.

'These are from Louis to you, Will,' she whispered. She thought of the woman in black, running away from her through the cemetery of graves. 'For you and the cousins and brothers and husbands and sons that are with you.'

The sun rose high overhead as Tiney pulled aside the barbed-wire coils and climbed onto the road again. As she walked through the sunshine, her shadow stretched out before her. In her mind's eye she made a picture of Louis and Will walking alongside her, their shadows overlapping. And for the first time since that morning at Larksrest, the morning when Papa had come into the room a changed man and Mama had spilt her basket of plums across the floor, Tiney felt at peace.

Butterfly kisses

Tiney stepped off the train at Friedrichstrasse, into the bustle of a Berlin afternoon. She'd slept much of the way from the Belgian border, where a customs officer had taken her papers and shouted at her until she explained, in her best German, that she had come to visit her cousin.

From Ypres Tiney had travelled to Brussels, where she spent three miserable nights in a hotel. She had made the mistake of detailing her travel plans in the note she had left Ida, and when she checked in at the front desk she was given a stack of mail forwarded from Paris. There was a letter from her parents, one from Thea and, most annoyingly, a long letter from Ida begging Tiney to come back to Paris. There was also a slim white envelope from Geneva.

Tiney placed the letters from her family and Ida in her suitcase. Then she sat up all night writing a reply to Martin. His letter was as honest and intimate as their conversation in the restaurant. Even if he wasn't interested in her romantically, at least she was sure he valued her friendship. She wrote back to him sharing every detail of her visit to Ypres and also gave him an outline of her planned visit to Berlin, though she knew he wouldn't approve.

Berlin was beautiful in the afternoon light, with its elegant buildings, shops with plate-glass windows, and tree-lined boulevards. Trams and buses glided smoothly along the streets. There were no ruins, no dust, and no destruction. The bombs had never reached Berlin. Unter den Linden, a long boulevard of trees budding with green leaves, lifted Tiney's heart for a moment but as she drew closer to Kurfürstendamm she began to notice that beneath the surface, the city was suffering. She saw a half-starved woman in black holding the hands of two skinny little children, and a barefooted girl with a wretched face leaning against the corner of a building dressed in nothing but her overcoat. Then Tiney passed a man standing on a street corner, begging. He had only one leg and one eye. The side of his head was bandaged with dirty strips of cloth. He held out a tin cup to passers-by, and Tiney could not bring herself to meet the gaze of his single blue eye.

Tiney was alarmed to find Hotel Elvira was both smaller and grubbier than she'd hoped. She checked in and then set off on her quest, crossing over the river into a network of narrow laneways, where the poverty of the city grew even more obvious. A pile of rags in the shadows of a deep doorway began to move and she saw the faces of an old woman and two small children peer out from amid the dirty cloth.

She stopped a girl, dressed in a tattered wool coat, and showed her the address that Onkel Ludwig had sent her, the address from which Paul had last written to his parents. The woman pointed down another shadowy laneway.

Inside the building, the paint was peeling from the walls and a bitter dampness hung in the air. Tiney climbed to the second floor and knocked on the door of the apartment. It opened only a crack and a dark eye peered out at her.

'*Guten Tag*,' she said, using her best German, 'I'm looking for Paul Kreiger. My name is Martina. I'm Paul's cousin from Australia.'

The door opened wide and a thin, dark-haired woman stared at Tiney, her face lit with wonder and surprise. 'Tiney Flynn!' she cried.

From behind her skirts, a fair-haired boy peered up at Tiney. For an instant, Tiney was confused. Had Paul married a widow? Who was this woman and her golden-haired child? And then she knew. This was the woman in Louis' photo, the woman holding the small baby, though the baby was now a boy.

'You know me?' said Tiney.

'Your cousin talked of you often. He told me about you and your sisters and your brother Louis. This little boy, my son, his name is Louis also,' she said, drawing the boy to stand shyly in front of her. 'He is named for your brother.'

Tiney couldn't think what it could mean. For a fleeting instance of longing, she wanted the boy to be Louis' son, to be her very own nephew. But how could it be possible? How could Louis have fathered a child that was raised behind enemy lines and never written of it? And the boy looked too old. Louis hadn't reached Europe until late in 1915, so no child of his could be older than four.

As if the young woman understood Tiney's confusion, she said, 'My name is Hannah. My son, his father is your cousin Wilhelm.'

Tiney felt her knees grow weak as she understood what the woman had told her. All the pieces of the jigsaw were falling into place. Hannah drew her through the open doorway and led her into the small apartment. It was simply a bedsit, with a bed in one corner, a long divan in another, a small table with three chairs, and one window overlooking the laneway. Hannah gestured for Tiney to sit down.

'Will is alive?' asked Tiney, hope and confusion brimming inside her. Could it be that he was not among the fallen at Langemarck?

Hannah hung her head. 'No,' she replied softly. 'No, he died when our child was a baby.'

'But my uncle sent me this address as Paul's address. Do my uncle and aunt know about you and the baby?'

'I'm not a baby,' interrupted Louis. 'I'm six years old!'

Hannah smiled and stroked the boy's fair hair. 'No,' she said. 'Wilhelm sent a picture of little Louis to your brother just before the war began. He was the only one who knew about our child until now, though Will also wrote to Paul and told him that we were engaged. Now Paul thinks it best not to tell your uncle and aunt. Not yet.'

'But you must tell them. You must!' said Tiney.

Hannah drew a deep breath. 'Australia is so far away. Until Paul came and found me in Heidelberg, I couldn't think of this family. I was Wilhelm's fiancée, but never his wife. At first, we couldn't marry because he was a student and I was a secret he kept from his parents. My father wouldn't have countenanced it either – Wilhelm was a foreigner, a gentile. I ran away from home to be with him. Then the war began. And we were going to marry when he was next on leave. But he never came back. He never lived to give me and our son his name, so I couldn't believe your uncle and aunt would accept me.'

Tiney didn't know what to say. How would her uncle and aunt feel about a child born out of wedlock?

Hannah made them tea and they sat and talked as the afternoon slipped into evening. Little Louis played quietly on the floor and listened. Finally, when the sky outside the window had darkened, Hannah lit the gas wall lamp. She insisted Tiney join her and Louis for their evening meal and went downstairs to warm a pot of turnip soup in her landlady's kitchen.

It was a simple, meagre meal and Tiney was embarrassed that she had arrived empty-handed. Louis scraped the bottom of his bowl and licked the spoon and Tiney offered him the rest of her soup, though she was still hungry.

Hannah was putting Louis to bed when the key turned in the lock and Paul stepped into the room. He frowned when he saw Tiney, almost as though he didn't recognise her.

'*Guten Abend*, Cousin Paul,' she said.

Then Paul crossed the room swiftly and enveloped her in a hug. Tiney pressed her face against his dark wool coat smelling of tobacco and soap and hugged him back. All her irritation with him evaporated and when he held her at arms-length to gaze into her face, she smiled.

'Did my parents send you?' he asked.

'Yes and no,' she answered. 'They paid my fare to Europe but they don't know that I'm here in Berlin.'

Paul visibly slumped. 'Then you haven't brought me any cash, have you?'

'What happened to your trust fund?' asked Tiney.

Paul glanced over at Hannah, who was sitting on the bed, gently humming a song to Louis as he drifted off to sleep.

'Let's go out for a walk,' he said. 'I'll escort you back to your accommodation. It's not a good idea for you to walk the streets alone.'

Tiney whispered a hurried goodbye to Hannah, promising to visit again tomorrow. Then she put on her hat and followed Paul out into the dark street.

'We must get you back to your hotel before curfew,' said Paul. 'Where are you staying?'

'In a pension in Kurfürstendamm,' said Tiney.

Paul looked surprised but said nothing. He seemed to be wrestling with what he wanted to say first.

'Why didn't you tell me, Paul?' asked Tiney. 'You knew, when I showed you the photo of Hannah and the baby, didn't you? You knew who they were, but you said nothing.'

'Will wrote to me from Heidelberg. He said he was in love with a woman, a Jewess called Hannah. He said he didn't think our parents would approve, more because he was too young and was still a student than because of her religion. He didn't tell me he was going to become a father. But when I saw the photo, that evening when you and I argued at Kaiserstuhl, I simply knew. She looked exactly as he'd described her in his letters. And if the photo was among Louis' things, it would have been because Will had sent it to him before August 1914, which matched the date on the back. Will trusted Louis more than me, I suppose.' Tiney heard a hint of Paul's familiar bitterness.

'Is that why you ran away? Because of the photo?' asked Tiney. 'But why didn't you tell me?'

'How could I? What if I was wrong? What if Hannah had married someone else and the child wasn't Will's? There was so much I couldn't know. And I wasn't sorry to leave, you know that.'

'But why are you living in such poverty? Paul, that room, it's not a fit place to raise a child.'

Paul hung his head. 'I could only get access to one part of the trust. My father controls the rest and he won't release it unless I come home.'

'But if you told him about Hannah and Louis, then surely he would help.'

The streetlights made Paul look pale and wan. 'I've found work in a nightclub, but everything is expensive when you've only got German marks and not foreign cash. I should have left Hannah and the boy in Heidelberg. But they were living in poverty there too. I thought I could offer them a better life here.'

'Are you in love with her?' asked Tiney.

Paul looked startled. 'No. But she's my sister-in-law in everything except name and Louis is my nephew. Wilhelm should have married her. He should have told our parents.'

'Then why haven't you told them?'

'They'd never believe me,' said Paul. 'They'd think I'm just trying to get my hands on the trust.'

'They'd believe you if they could see Louis. He looks so much like Will. No one could see him and not realise that he's Will's son.'

Paul didn't reply but kept walking swiftly along the avenue. Kurfürstendamm at night was a different landscape. Cafes and bars cast golden light onto the pavement. Girls with painted faces and short skirts stood along the roadside.

Tiney pointed to the entrance of Hotel Elvira. 'That's where I'm staying,' she said.

Paul groaned. 'You can't be serious! What made you choose that flophouse?'

'A friend of Ida's in Paris stayed there before the war,' said Tiney, feeling embarrassed.

'Berlin was a different city before the war. We'll get your suitcase and I'll take you back to Hannah's. I have to get to work soon and we both need to be off the streets before midnight. There's still a curfew in place because of the putsch and the general strike.'

When Tiney asked for her suitcase at the pension's reception, she found the lock on it had been broken and the contents rifled through. Paul cursed the porter but Tiney didn't want to make a fuss. She was glad she'd carried all her cash and papers in her handbag.

Back out in the street, a group of women called out angrily to Tiney and Paul.

'What did they say?' asked Tiney, confused by their heavy accents.

'They think I'm your pimp and we're encroaching on their territory,' said Paul.

'They're women of the night?' asked Tiney, her voice squeaky with surprise. 'They think I'm one too? Me?'

'There are tens of thousands trying to sell themselves. How else can they feed their children?'

As they came to the next corner, a tall man stepped out of the darkness and Paul attempted to cross the road to avoid him. But the tall man quickened his pace and began to follow them. Tiney heard Paul mutter a curse under his breath.

'Walk faster and don't look back,' said Paul. But they could hear the man's footsteps drawing nearer. Tiney glanced over her shoulder and saw the man gesturing them to slow down.

'Don't look back!' said Paul.

Finally, in exasperation, Paul turned to face the man and spoke to him roughly in German. Tiney kept her head down.

'I'm sorry to disturb you,' said the man in English. 'I thought…'

As his voice trailed off, Tiney looked up in disbelief.

'Martin?' she said. 'What are you doing here?'

'Tiney! It is you!' said Martin, his face awash with relief.

Tiney quickly introduced Paul to Martin, stumbling as she tried to explain their complicated connection, until Martin intervened.

'Your cousin wrote and told me she was coming to Berlin,' he said to Paul. Then he turned to Tiney. 'As soon as I got your letter, I set out from Geneva. They told me you'd checked in at Hotel Elvira so I waited for you to come back. I didn't mean to startle you.'

Paul tapped his foot and glanced at his wristwatch, and Tiney realise this was not the right place, not the right time, to explain. Tiney arranged to meet Martin the next day and set off again with Paul.

Suddenly Paul laughed. 'You know, little cousin,' he said, 'I have always underestimated you. Our whole family has underestimated you. We should have known that surprising things can come in quite small packages.'

Tiney was dreaming. A butterfly had landed on her face and its soft wings were kissing her cheek. She opened her eyes to see early-morning light filtering through the window of Hannah's apartment. Little Louis, who had slept between her and Hannah, was sitting up in bed and staring at her. His small hand stroked her cheek.

'*Guten Morgen, meine süße winzige kleine Tante,*' he said.

Tiney smiled. No one had ever called her their darling, tiny little aunt before. She sat up and gazed at him, this elfin boy she almost felt she'd dreamt into being.

'*Guten Morgen, mein hübscher Neffe,*' she said, touching his small chin gently. Louis grinned and flung his arms around her neck.

She lifted him out of bed and tiptoed across the room with the boy in her arms. Paul had returned at dawn and was asleep on the divan. Louis and Tiney sat at the small table by the window, talking in whispers so as not to wake the others. Tiney told him about Australia, about his cousins in Adelaide and his grandparents in the Barossa Valley. Louis told her of his friends from the lane, of the games they played and his favourite things to eat. Before Paul and Hannah woke, Tiney and Louis crept out of the apartment and wandered into the Berlin morning to buy *Frühstück* for their family: *Schrippen* with golden crusts as well as dark, seedy rolls, a lump of salty butter, some jam, a hunk of cheese and a pot of fresh *Kräuterquark*. Louis laughed and peered into the brown-paper bag.

'*Danke, kleine Tante,*' he said.

Holding hands, they climbed the narrow stairs of the tenement.

Staircase to the moon

Early next evening, Martin arrived to collect Tiney from the tenement. The whole lane stopped to stare at the man on the British motorcycle, in his brown leather jacket and black cap.

Tiney tried not to cling to Martin as the Royal Enfield sped out into the wide Berlin avenue, but when the motorcycle dipped deeply as he turned a corner, she couldn't help but wrap her arms around him and hold fast.

They drove down the wide boulevards and then into small and winding streets to arrive at the club where Paul worked as a pianist. Lamps flickered to life, illuminating the streets and casting deep shadows. Women stood on the roadside in pools of golden light.

Inside, the club was smoky and smelt of stale beer. As it was still early in the evening and there was only a sprinkling of patrons, Tiney was embarrassed she'd suggested it. They sat in a booth at the back, leaning their heads together so as to be able to hear each other speak over the voices of scantily clad singers. The club served little food but Tiney wasn't hungry. She hardly touched the platter of bread, sausage and pickles that Martin had ordered. She simply wanted to drink in the sound of

235

Martin's voice and to tell him everything.

'My cousin says he doesn't want to leave Berlin,' said Tiney. 'He says he loves the city, that it makes him feel alive; but they're living in terrible circumstances.'

Martin leaned closer, trying to hear her over the band. Then he put his mouth close to her ear. 'Let's not talk about your cousin any longer,' he said. 'Or the war or the past or anything that makes you unhappy. I'd like to take you dancing.'

The dance hall had a small garden, delicate with spring flowers, at the entrance.

'It's not what it seems,' said Martin. They climbed a flight of stairs and passed through a labyrinth of hallways. The smell of smoke and beer, sweat, powder and perfume drifted down to encompass them. As they waited in the queue outside the cloakroom, Martin took Tiney's coat, and her bare shoulders tingled in the cool spring air. She touched her bobbed hair and knew she looked as stylish as any of the other dancers.

Martin took her hand and led her into a grand room with long, gilt-edged mirrors on the walls. The glass was speckled and their image seemed foggy as they whirled across the marble floor. Gaslight flickered in the mirrors, cigarette smoke swirled above their heads and the band played all the new songs from America, a trumpeter blasting out a wailing solo above the other instruments. As they danced, it was as if Tiney was watching someone from another era, a time before the war or perhaps far into the future, when every unhappiness had been forgotten. She looked up smiling into Martin's face and saw an answering look of pleasure in his eyes.

After more than an hour of dancing, Martin led her from the dance floor. 'There's one other place I want to show you tonight,' he said. 'We'll visit it in the daylight tomorrow, but it's just as beautiful at night.'

The motorcycle thrummed beneath them as they rode through the Berlin streets. Tiney heard gunfire from the city rooftops but she shut her eyes and breathed deeply of the night air. She wouldn't be afraid, not now, not after all the miles she had travelled to reach this moment. Curfew was fast approaching and Martin revved the motorcycle as they turned into the darkness of the Tiergarten, the vast parkland in the centre of Berlin. The trees were black, the forest thick and dark with dappled patches of moonlight shining through the canopy of spring leaves. Martin stopped the bike beside a fountain, not far from a lake of shimmering water.

'This is the loveliest place in Berlin by moonlight,' he said. 'War can ruin many things but it can't spoil moonlight on water. Even when the fighting was at its worst in the Somme, moonlight on water made me remember that the world was bigger than a battlefield.'

Tiney slipped from the motorcycle and Martin took her hand and led her to the water's edge where a shimmering staircase of moonlight stretched across the lake.

'It's beautiful,' said Tiney.

They stood side by side in the stillness. Then Martin turned to her. He put one finger beneath her chin and tilted her face up to the stars before he bent down to kiss her lips. It was the softest, most fleeting kiss, but for a moment Tiney felt suspended in air, floating above the surface of the earth, as if she were a swan about to take flight across the moonlit lake.

Then Martin stepped away and she felt the space between them.

'Martina Flynn,' he said.

'Martin Woolf,' she answered, and they both laughed.

As they rode back through Berlin, past the Brandenburg Gate, speeding through the darkening streets, Tiney's skirt rippled out behind her in the breeze. She pressed her cheek firmly against Martin's back and knew, as certain as moonlight on water, as sure as the touch of a butterfly wing on her cheek, that everything was just beginning.

18 November 1923

Tiney reached out to help Ray Junior down from the tram. He looked shyly to either side, not sure of his strange new aunt, and then he jumped to land beside her.

Martin helped Mama step down from the tram. She had grown thinner and frailer in the years Tiney had been away.

'He's quite the gentleman, your Martin,' said Nette, as they strolled towards Glenelg Beach.

Tiney smiled. Martin was walking ahead with Louis, Onkel Ludwig and Papa. As the sea came into view, they all stopped to admire the blue water of the Gulf of St Vincent. Louis had grown close to Martin on the voyage back from Europe and now he held Martin's hand as he chatted shyly to his grandfather and great-uncle in German.

Glenelg Beach was already crowded with families. Across the white sand, small tents were sprouting. Women sat beneath black umbrellas, crowds of small children paddled in the shallows and couples wandered along the jetty hand in hand. Sunlight glittered on the surface of the sea.

While Frank and Ray set up a small striped canvas tent for shade, Nette, Minna and Thea unpacked the picnic baskets and spread out a tartan rug on the warm beach. Minna and Frank's baby girl sat placidly eating handfuls of sand, until Tiney picked her up and wiped her pink cheeks.

'Do you think we can make the tent private enough for us all to change into our bathing suits or shall we hire a bathing box?' asked Thea.

'Oh, let's just change in the tent,' said Tiney.

'That's all right for you, Miss Flynn,' said Nette, patting the swell of her pregnant belly. ' I couldn't possibly fit in there.'

'You're not swimming in your condition!' said Mama.

'We're taking Louis in for his first swim in the ocean,' said Tiney, reaching one hand out to Martin.

'Lucky that they've finally allowed mixed bathing,' said Minna. 'But you do know you can't wear a one-piece bathing costume?'

Tiney laughed. 'Don't worry, I haven't turned completely European.'

She slipped into the tent and wriggled into her blue sailor bathing costume, tugging at the skirt to make it look a little longer.

The men in their Sunday best sat in the sand, their hats tipped back. Hannah sat beside Tiney, still shy of all her newly discovered relations.

'Are you coming in or not?' Tiney called as she and Martin walked down to the water's edge.

Louis looked shyly from his mother to his aunt.

'Go on, *liebling*,' said Hannah. 'Tante Tiney and Onkel Martin will be with you. The ocean is not so different to rivers and lakes.'

Louis, all long white limbs, ran down to the water's edge. Little Ray ran after him to stand in the shallows, admiring his big cousin.

Martin, Louis and Tiney walked into the clear, still water. The tide was out and even twenty yards from shore, the water was only waist deep. Martin let Louis climb onto his shoulders and leap into the air. Tiney looked up and watched as Louis jumped, suspended for a split second against the bright sky before he plunged into the sparkling water.

Tiney stretched her arms out to Louis as he rose out of the sea, laughing. He made his way towards her, catching hold of her hands, pulling her under. Martin dived in beside her. They splashed and laughed and then turned onto their backs to float on the calm blue of Holdfast Bay. Martin's hand brushed against hers and Louis kicked a silvery spray of seawater into the air. Tiney looked up at the sky above her, like the vault of heaven, and sighed with happiness.

Acknowledgements

I am grateful to the Australia Council for its support of this project, the Wheeler Centre for its Hot Desk Fellowship and The May Gibbs Trust for its Canberra Fellowship. I am indebted to the State Library of Victoria, the State Library of South Australia, the Australian War Memorial Research Centre, the Tanunda Public Library and the Commonwealth Graves Commission in Ypres for their assistance and invaluable resources. Many people provided support, hospitality and advice from Adelaide to Berlin during the writing and researching of this novel, including Robyn Annear, Mary Hoyle, Julie Walker, Stuart Gluth, Cat Fletcher, Natta Jain, Lesley Reece, Ruby J. Murray, Ken Harper, Billy Murray, Christian von Raumer, Sarah Brenan and Susannah Chambers. Countless books and resources underpinned the writing of this novel but I'd particularly like to acknowledge the poems of Mary Gilmore; the papers of Jessie Traill; Jane Tolerton's biograpy of Ettie Rout, *Ettie*; and the works of Joy Damousi, Bart Ziino, Mat McLachlan, Chris Ilert and Ken Inglis. This novel includes brief excerpts from Mary Gilmore's poems 'These Fellowing Men' and 'Inheritance', an excerpt from Adam Lindsay Gordon's poem 'Ars Longa (A Song of Pilgrimage)' and an excerpt from two works by Johann Wolfgang von Goethe, *Hermann And Dorothea – VI. Klio* and *Wilhelm Meisters Wanderjahre*.

Author's Note

In February 2010, the bodies of 250 Australian soldiers were reinterred in a specially constructed Military Cemetery at Fromelles (Pheasant Wood). The mothers, sisters, wives, lovers and girlfriends of these men are all dead too. They lie in graves across Australia. They died after a lifetime of contribution to their communities. The stories of their fortitude and suffering in the face of grief are largely forgotten. Thinking of all those women and how they are so often overlooked in Australian history and fiction inspired me to write *The Year It All Ended*, to refocus the historical lens on the people who are left out of the picture.

My family, like many Australian families, was deeply affected by World War I. Although *The Year It All Ended* is a work of fiction I drew on a large body of family history to flesh out the characters of the Flynn family and their community. The youngest of my great-aunts, Agnes 'Lit' MacNamara, was the inspiration for Tiney Flynn. Like Tiney, she was born on the 11th of November, 1901 and was the littlest member of her family (hence her nickname 'Lit'). Aunty Lit was an adventuress who travelled extensively, including a trip down the Amazon River on a tramp steamer. She told me many stories about growing up in Adelaide during the war years and about the death of her only brother, Louis, on the Western Front. She longed to visit his grave and did eventually get there but not as quickly as Tiney. Unlike Tiney, Aunty Lit never found romantic love but in this novel, I wanted to give her an ending that she would have loved to have lived. One of the great pleasures in writing fiction is imaginatively resolving the suffering of your characters without distorting history.

History, as written, often focuses on violence. We read it as a sequence of interconnected acts of aggression. But history as lived is a tapestry of daily rituals; of eating, cleaning, studying, playing, nurturing, working, loving and grieving – of small pleasures and large emotional challenges. The history of living is a story of the interconnectedness of families, friends and lovers; the things that matter in the lives of every single human being.